Sam jumped up.
"God, are we boring or what?

Here we are, three incredibly fine babes on vacation, and we're sitting in a hotel room moaning and groaning. Let's go find some fun! Let's go get wild!"

"I thought you had two shows to do," Emma said.

"True," Sam agreed. "But after that, the sky is the limit! No cute guy in Orlando is safe tonight!" she predicted. "Why, you may ask?"

"Why?" Carrie and Emma asked on cue.

"Because we rule!" Sam crowed. She checked her watch. "Wow, gotta boogie. Listen, just hop on the monorail in about a half-hour. Ask at the information center for the Rocking Fifties Revue. Here, I got some passes for you. You can't miss me. I'll be the incredibly cute redhead dancing in the second row who deserves to get discovered!"

Sam flew towards the door, but stopped suddenly and turned back to her two friends. "I'm just so glad you guys are here, you know?"

The happiness on Carrie's and Emma's faces was the only answer Sam needed.

Sunset Reunion

CHERIE BENNETT

SPLASH™

A BERKLEY / SPLASH BOOK

This book is for Jeff

ONE

Emma reached out and pulled Kurt to her, running her hands through his sun-bleached hair as she planted hot kisses on his lips.

"I'll never let anything come between us again," Kurt vowed, burying his face in her fragrant hair.

"I know," Emma whispered, letting her hands roam down Kurt's muscled back. "Kurt, I want to—"

"Ladies and gentlemen, we're beginning our descent into Orlando," came the pilot's deep, melodious voice over the speaker startling Emma Cresswell awake. *Poof!* Gone just like that, was Kurt and the incredible dream she'd been having about him.

"The temperature in Orlando is a sunny seventy-eight degrees this afternoon," the pilot continued. "We'll be landing in about ten minutes. Thank you for flying Delta Airlines."

"We're here!" Carrie Alden said from the seat next to Emma. She squeezed Emma's arm with excitement and peered out the window as the pilot dipped the plane toward its landing.

Emma smiled at Carrie and tried to catch a glimpse of the ground over her friend's shoulder. It was much more difficult than it would have been in first class, Emma noted. This was the very first time that Emma had flown anything *but* first class, actually. Well, she couldn't very well have told Carrie that she was going to buy her usual first-class ticket and meet her once they landed.

"I'm so pumped for this," Carrie said happily. "I've never been to Disney World before. Can you believe that Sam, our Samantha Bridges, is actually working there as a professional dancer? It's really unbelievable!"

Emma laughed. "You know Sam. With her we should always expect the unexpected!"

And it really *had* been unexpected.

At the end of the summer it had been horrible for the three of them to say goodbye to Sunset Island and to one another.

They had become so close over the three months they spent there that it was hard to believe there had ever been a time when they hadn't been best friends.

As the plane descended Emma and Carrie both thought back to their final night together on the island. Emma, Carrie, and Sam had gone to the beach and sat on the rocks watching the sun set over the water. Each had contemplated that final sunset and all the changes that had taken place in their lives.

Emma had felt unsettled about both her love life and her plans for the future. Though she'd learned a lot about herself during her summer as an au pair on Sunset Island—almost more than she wanted to know, she reflected wryly—nothing about her life seemed resolved at all. She'd fallen in love with a hunky local guy, Kurt Ackerman, early in the summer. It was the first time she'd ever experienced that special feeling for someone, but as much as they cared for each other, it seemed that their backgrounds kept getting in the way— Kurt's family was poor and Emma's family was rich. They had finally, painfully, broken up, but Emma still felt that she loved Kurt, and she believed that he loved her, too. And as much as she had been trying to get interested in other guys, it was still Kurt who she dreamed about, Kurt who occupied her thoughts.

And then there was her future. Emma longed to tell her parents that she wasn't much interested in living the lifestyle of a Boston heiress, that she didn't want to attend elite Goucher College and study French, as they expected her to do. How could she tell them that what she really wanted was to join the Peace Corps? She'd thought about it a lot during the summer on Sunset Island, but as yet hadn't done a thing about it except dream. For all the growing up she'd done over the summer, Emma was still scared that deep down inside she might be nothing more than a spoiled rich girl who couldn't stand up to a real challenge.

Carrie's plans for the future, by contrast, had seemed more certain on that August evening. Always an excellent student, Carrie would be going to Yale in the fall. She'd dreamed for years of becoming a professional photojournalist, maybe even a documentary filmmaker, and she was certain that studying at Yale would be an incredible experience that would also help her achieve her goal.

When Carrie considered her love life, however, things seemed a bit more confusing. She had fallen hard for Billy Sampson, the lead singer of the local rock group Flirting with Danger. At first she had thought that maybe she just liked Billy's attention. After all, Billy was incredibly sexy—every girl on the island seemed to lust after him—and Carrie saw herself as the girl-next-door type, not the type to be a rock star's girlfriend. In fact, she had even thought she would have to change for him. But as they'd gotten to know each other better, Carrie had realized that they really did have a lot in common, much more than just a physical attraction. The fact of the matter was that she was really crazy about him, and the same seemed to be true for him, since they had wound up being an item for most of the summer. On the other hand, Carrie had been corresponding with her ex-boyfriend, Josh, from back home in New Jersey, and she wasn't sure just what they were to each other any more. She didn't feel the real physical pull toward him that she felt for Billy, but on the other hand she and Josh were so in tune with each other that Carrie couldn't bear not to have Josh be a part of her life. And Josh was pretty adamant that he wanted more than just Carrie's friendship.

As for Sam, by the end of the summer she had still seemed to be the most adrift of the three of them. During the summer she had gone out with Presley, the bass player from the Flirts, but it hadn't ever turned into a big romance like the ones Emma and Carrie had had. Lots of guys had flirted with Sam—being a tall, thin, gorgeous redhead had its advantages—and she was an expert extraordinaire at flirting back. But when it came to real love, Sam knew she had not even come close yet. It bothered her that her knowledge of guys was mostly just theory, and she longed to fall madly in love with someone. Unfortunately, the right someone hadn't come along yet.

Sam had won a full dance scholarship to Kansas State, which in her small Kansas town was a very big deal. Her parents had been thrilled to no end. It had not been, however, a big deal to Sam. She had longed to bypass what she thought of as four years of academic grind and move right on to the lifestyle of the rich and famous. Surely with her looks, nerve, and natural talent as a dancer, all she needed was the right person to come along and discover her. But, Sam had figured, Kansas State wasn't a likely spot in which to be discovered.

Sam, Carrie, and Emma all had dreams they wanted to fulfill. Their dreams were what they had in common. Only it was one thing to dream and quite another to make the dreams come true.

As the sun had disappeared beyond the horizon that last night on Sunset Island, they'd all wondered what would become of them, and of their friendship, now that it was time to move on.

"I just can't believe I have to leave you guys," Sam had said, staring out at the water.

Emma and Carrie both had had lumps in their throats. They'd felt the same way. Then Carrie, always the practical one, had come up with the reunion idea.

"Why don't we get together for Christmas vacation?" she had suggested. "That's not so far away."

"What a great idea!" Emma had cried. "And no matter what happens to us between now and then, we can be sure we'll be together again in just four months."

"Four months!" Sam had wailed, throwing herself back onto the cool sand. "Four months is a lifetime!"

"I bet it passes really quickly," Carrie had told her. "Where do you think we should meet?"

"Paris?" Sam had suggested hopefully.

"Well, why not right here?" Emma had said. "It will be the off season, so there will be plenty of room at the Sunset Inn." In the back of Emma's mind had been the fact that it would mean being near Kurt again, though she could hardly even admit that to herself.

They'd all agreed—a Christmas reunion on Sunset Island it would be. Planning the reunion had made it a little easier to say good-bye the next day because they knew they'd be together again soon.

Emma had headed off to Goucher, just as her parents expected, feeling like a complete hypocrite for not standing up to them. Carrie had taken to Yale like a duck to water, and had written excited letters to both Emma and Sam telling them how fabulous Yale was. And it had been impetuous Sam who changed her plans completely.

She had registered at Kansas State and had already attended two weeks of classes when she'd seen the ad in the local paper. The headline read, "Local Auditions Slated for Singers and Dancers for Disney World." Sam had quickly read the rest of the ad. It had explained that Disney World held regional auditions all over the country to find the best and most enthusiastic young singers and dancers for the famous theme park. The auditions were to be at a local dance club two days later. Sam had immediately vowed she would be there.

Evidently a lot of other people in town had had the same idea, because Sam had been number eighty-seven when she arrived. Sam had had to take a deep breath, but she knew she looked great in her hot pink leotard and glitter tights, and she'd danced her little heart out for the judges. She could tell they liked her dancing, so she hadn't felt too self-conscious when they asked her to sing. She wasn't much of a singer, but she could carry a tune, so she had just belted out a song and hoped for the best.

As if in a fairy tale, for once the best actually happened. A week later Sam had gotten a call at her dorm offering her a job as a dancer at Disney World. They had told her they would pay to fly her to Orlando, and pay her a salary and everything, just like a professional dancer. They had told her to take a few days and think seriously about whether or not she wanted to leave school to take the job. Sam had thought about it for about five seconds. As far as she was concerned, four of those seconds had been wasted time.

So that was how plans for the big reunion had changed locales from Sunset Island to Orlando, where Disney World was. It hadn't been hard for Sam to convince Carrie and Emma that they should come there. Carrie had had some money saved from the photos she'd sold to a rock magazine, and Emma of course could afford to go wherever she wanted, whenever she wanted. The girls had planned it so that Carrie and Emma would get to see Sam do her shows. Then Sam would take a few days off and they would all live it up.

"Basically, we'll just have great adventures, break hearts, and party," Sam had told Emma on the phone the night before she left for Florida. Emma had laughed, but she knew that with Sam anything was possible.

On the morning of their flight Carrie had caught a ride with a friend to New York City, where Emma had been staying with her Aunt Liz since her Christmas break began a few days earlier. She and Carrie had talked nonstop on their way to the airport and on the plane. Now they were finally about to land, and all three girls would be reunited at last.

The wheels touched down on the runway, and Carrie and Emma turned to each other, both grinning from ear to ear.

"This is going to be fabulous," Carrie predicted.

"When you're right, you're right," Emma agreed. "Florida may never be the same."

"*We* may never be the same," Carrie added with a laugh.

"Good," Emma said. "I, for one, am ready for anything."

Carrie raised her eyebrows at Emma as the plane taxied toward the terminal. "Anything?" she asked. "Aren't you supposed to add 'within reason' or 'that my parents would approve of,' or something like that?"

"*Anything*," Emma repeated firmly.

Both girls undid their safety belts and stood up to get their bags from the overhead compartment. "Emma," Carrie said, reaching for her bag, "I like the way you think. Sunny Florida, here we come!"

TWO

"Eeeeeeeeeeek!" Sam screamed happily when she saw Emma and Carrie walking toward her in the airport. Sam jumped up and down with excitement, waving at them maniacally. Next to five-foot-ten Sam was a seven-foot-tall Goofy, also jumping up and down and waving with equal happiness.

"Omigod, I can't believe you guys are really here!" Sam screamed as she enveloped both Carrie and Emma in a three-way bear hug. Goofy wrapped his long arms around all three of them.

"That's enough, Danny," Sam told Goofy. Goofy stepped back good-naturedly. "This is my friend Danny Franklin," Sam told her friends. "He plays Goofy at Disney World."

"So we see," said Emma, grinning at Goofy. Goofy waved at her.

"I missed you guys so much!" Sam said, hugging them both again. Goofy moved to join in. "Please," Sam snorted at him, which stopped him short. Somehow, even through his Goofy face, he managed to look crestfallen.

"Don't you talk?" Carrie asked him, peering up at him. Goofy shrugged.

"He thinks it's method acting or something," Sam said, rolling her eyes. "See, when he's playing Goofy at Disney World he can't talk, so he refuses to talk whenever he's wearing his Goofy outfit," she explained.

"I see," said Emma, who was biting her lip to keep from laughing.

Sam turned to Goofy. "Danny, how about you go get the van and bring it around to the door by the baggage pickup?" she suggested. "We'll meet you there."

Goofy put his hands on his hips and looked at Sam as if he was angry.

"I'm sorry, Goofy," Sam said. "I didn't mean to call you Danny."

Goofy nodded happily and loped off toward the exit.

Emma, Carrie, and Sam stared at one

another for a second, and then all three of them burst out laughing.

"Only you, Sam," Carrie said, wiping the tears from her eyes.

"What can I say? He's in love with me, he takes me everywhere," Sam said with a sigh. "He's got this great van, and I'm too poor to afford a car yet, so he's kind of useful."

"Sam!" Emma reproached her, shaking her head. "How can you lead poor Goofy on?"

"I kind of like him, actually," Sam said, shrugging. "Anyhow, as you will see, he is to-die-for cute underneath that costume. The only problem is that he's really shy, so he feels more comfortable when he's Goofy than when he's Danny."

"I'd be shy if I were seven feet tall, too," Emma said.

"No, he's only a little over six feet tall, really," Sam explained as they headed toward the baggage carousels. "His eyes are looking out of Goofy's mouth." She surveyed her two best friends happily. "I'm so glad to see you guys. You both look so great!"

"So do you," Carrie told Sam. "But then you always look great."

Sam had on a short full black cotton skirt with a Day–Glo green crinoline petticoat peeking out from underneath it. With it she wore a black T-shirt trimmed with lace. On her feet were her trademark red cowboy boots.

"Thanks," Sam said, spinning around for them. She scrutinized Carrie again. "Something's different about you, though, Carrie. What is it?"

"I think she lost weight," Emma said, transferring her overnight bag to her other shoulder.

"But I didn't," Carrie said.

"I know what it is!" Sam said, stopping in her tracks. "You're not wearing baggy clothes! You look just incredible!"

Carrie grinned. Her friends had tried to convince her all summer that she should stop trying to hide her curvy figure under baggy, oversized T-shirts and pants, but Carrie had felt too self-conscious to listen to them. Somehow being at Yale had given her confidence, and she'd recently started wearing the occasional miniskirt, or a top that skimmed her torso instead of hiding it. Today she had on a white sleeveless cotton mock turtleneck with snug-fitting blue jeans.

Sam spun her around and whistled. "Get down, girl, you are hot!"

"Well, I'll never be a size five," Carrie said, "but I'm getting more okay about it."

"We all can't be as perfectly petite as Emma," Sam said, craning her neck to see if the luggage was arriving yet.

Emma smiled. *Same old Sam*, she thought. There was simply no censor between Sam's brain and her mouth. Emma had learned that Sam meant nothing hostile by her comments. In fact, if anything, Emma had learned to lighten up because of those comments, and at the beginning of the summer, she had really needed to do exactly that. She had just never had the opportunity to be around ordinary people.

"Speaking of perfect," Sam continued, checking out the paisley tapestry vest that Emma wore over a tank top, "that vest is killer."

"Thanks," Emma said, sweeping her perfect blond hair behind one diamond-studded ear. "I got it in SoHo a couple of days ago. I went on this outrageous shopping spree with my Aunt Liz."

"And spent outrageous bucks, no doubt," Sam said with a sigh. "I'm telling you, being poor sucks."

"But you're earning money at Disney World, aren't you?" Carrie asked. "I can't believe that you're actually a professional dancer now!" she added.

"Yeah, it's great," Sam said. "But as you can imagine, my parents just about gave birth when I called and told them I left school to take this job. They won't subsidize me one penny unless I go back to school, so I actually have to live on the money I make."

"There's my duffel bag," Carrie said, pointing to an olive-green bag that was moving toward them on the carousel.

"I'll grab it," Sam said, reaching her long arms out to scoop up the bag.

"You mean you called them on the telephone to tell them you had already left school?" Emma asked Sam. "You didn't even discuss it with them before you dropped out?"

"Of course not," Sam said. "They would have killed me. I didn't call them until I had signed the contract and flown to Florida. Then it was too late for them to stop me."

"You realize don't you," said Carrie, "that it's just possible that someday you will have a daughter just like you who will make your life miserable?"

"Puh-*leeze*." Sam shuddered. "Don't talk

to me about kids. I don't intend to have any. They're a royal pain."

"There's my suitcase," Emma said, ducking in front of a heavyset man to reach for her designer luggage.

"Is that everything?" Sam asked. Carrie and Emma nodded. "Should I get Danny to come haul this stuff? He's probably where he can't leave the car, but I could switch places with him," she offered.

"I'm okay," Carrie said.

"Me, too," Emma said, lifting her suitcase. Sam grabbed the handle to help her. "Okay, then, let's boogie!"

Goofy was lolling against the side of a black van painted with various stars, flowers, abstract designs, and scrawled slogans. The girls threw all their stuff in the back of the van and scrambled in. Danny crawled into the back and pulled off the head portion of his costume so he could see to drive.

"What did I tell you?" Sam said, turning around and giving her friends a significant look. "He's not really supposed to be out here in costume, but he insisted. What could I say?"

Sam, as usual, had been right. Danny really was to-die-for cute. His shaggy brown hair had streaks of auburn in it, and sea-green eyes peered out of a tanned and handsome face.

"Doesn't it get hot under there?" Carrie asked him as he started the van.

"A little," he admitted in a low voice.

"Shy," Sam mouthed at them, and shrugged. "Listen, I got you guys a room at the greatest hotel. It's so cool—the monorail that runs through Disney World stops inside, practically in front of your door!"

Emma had insisted on paying for the hotel, and Carrie had finally capitulated. The truth of the matter was that Emma didn't want to stay at a hotel out in the hinterlands, which is all Carrie would have been able to afford. Hotel prices were very, very high anywhere around there. Besides, Sam would be staying with them a lot—she described her rented room as being the size of a closet.

"Palm trees," Carrie sighed, leaning out the window of the van so that the breeze could ruffle her hair. "I love palm trees!"

"When do we get to see your show?" Emma asked Sam.

"Tonight," Sam promised. "I do the Rocking Fifties Revue at seven, and the Wild West Revue at eight."

"She's really great," Danny said, stopping at a light. "I mean, she's the best dancer. She really stands out."

Sam made a face. "Well, thanks, but I'm not supposed to stand out, so that probably isn't very good. I'm supposed to look exactly like the other five girls who are dancing with me."

"So do you love it?" Carrie asked.

"Sometimes," she answered. "Sometimes it's so exciting I have to pinch myself. Then sometimes I think I will just die if I have to look perky for one more second. They're very into perky there," she explained. Just then they pulled into the circular drive in front of a huge, marble-fronted hotel.

"Wow," Carrie breathed.

A uniformed doorman opened the door to the van and helped Sam from the front seat, then held out his hand to assist Emma and Carrie.

"You can get the bags out of the back," Sam told an approaching bellhop.

Danny jumped out of the van and started to put his Goofy head back on.

"How about leaving it off?" Sam suggested, her hand resting lightly on his fore-arm.

He gave her a lovesick look. "Okay," he agreed. "Actually, I should get back to work." He turned to Emma and Carrie. "Nice meeting you. I'll see you at the show tonight," he promised.

"Okay. And thanks for the lift!" Carrie yelled as Danny hopped back into the van.

"He's really sweet," Emma told Sam as they followed the bellhop into the lobby.

"But broke," Sam sighed. "I ask you, why is it always the broke guys who are so cute?"

Emma smiled ruefully. Kurt was broke, too. And though it hadn't really mattered to her, because she certainly didn't have to worry about money, she had to admit that it had been a burden on their relationship because *he* had cared.

It didn't take long to register—Sam stared covetously at Emma's gold American Express card when she whipped it out—and the girls followed the bellhop up to their room.

"Anything else I can get for you girls?" the young, clean-cut bellhop asked after he'd brought their bags in.

"No, that's fine," Emma said, handing him a tip. He gave Emma a dazzling smile.

"Okay, then. Have a great time here at the Magic Kingdom!"

He closed the door behind him as Carrie ran to open the sliding glass doors that led to a balcony. "Wow, come look at this! I can see all of Disney World from here! Oh, I love it!"

Emma ran to join her, and the two girls exclaimed over the fabulous view. Meanwhile, Sam bounced up and down on one of the beds—after all, she saw the place six days a week.

"All the bushes down there are trimmed in the shape of giant animals!" Emma said as she came back into the room.

"It kind of makes me wish I had a little kid with me," Carrie said wistfully. "Wouldn't you just love to show all this to some kid?"

"That's exactly why the old Magic Kingdom rakes in the big bucks," Sam said. "Every adult in the world wants to bring their kid here—or any kid here, for that matter."

"I can't wait to see it all!" Carrie said, plopping down on the other bed.

"It really is terrific here, I have to admit," Sam said with a grin.

"So, tell us all about it!" Emma coaxed. She sat cross-legged on the bed next to Sam.

"Well, I was so nervous when I first got here," Sam admitted, picking some red polish off the nail on her pinky. "I mean, I guess I'm a good dancer—"

"You're a great dancer!" Carrie interrupted.

"Thanks for the vote of confidence," Sam said, "but I didn't know if I could really compete with actual professionals."

"Evidently they thought so, though, or they wouldn't have hired you," Emma pointed out.

"Yeah, that's what I keep telling myself. I've worked really hard, and I'm doing okay, I guess, but sometimes I just feel like a cog in the wheel. . . ."

Carrie and Emma just stared at her.

"Like a robot could do what I'm doing!" Sam said earnestly. "Now and then I think they just hired me because they needed a redhead, and any old redhead tall enough to dance in the second row would do."

"I think you're selling yourself short," Emma said.

"Yeah," Carrie agreed. "Besides, this is only the very beginning of your career as a dancer. It takes a lot of dedication, a lot of sweat and hard work—"

"But I want it to happen *now!*" Sam said. "Some girls just get discovered. I don't see why it shouldn't be me!"

"*You're* the one who can make it happen," Carrie counseled, "not some mystical unknown person who would 'discover' you."

"That's true," Emma agreed. "Remember how much trouble that kind of thinking got you into with Flash Hathaway?"

Sam winced. Flash Hathaway was a big-time photographer who freelanced for Universal Models, one of the largest modeling agencies in the country. He had "discovered" Sam, and said he could make her into a superstar model. Sam had been so dazzled by the possibility that against her better judgment she had posed for him wearing some skimpy lingerie. She had believed the photos were only for her portfolio until she found out that Flash was exhibiting them at a local bar as if they were soft-core porn. And if that wasn't bad enough, when he had hired Sam for her very first professional modeling job he'd expected her to sleep with him as part of the deal. Fortunately Sam had gotten herself out of that one, but it had been a close call.

Sam lifted her masses of curly red hair off

her neck. "I hate it when the two of you are so practical. It's so . . . it's so . . ." Sam searched for the right word.

"Smart!" Emma finished for her with a laugh.

"I was thinking more along the lines of dull, boring, or sort of fossilized," Sam remarked. "Anyway, I want to hear what's going on with the two of you before I have to go get ready for the show. I hope one of you has a hot love life going so I can hear all the juicy details."

"Billy came up to Yale to see me last week," Carrie admitted with a small smile.

"Get out of here!" Sam yelled. "That's awesome!"

"Kind of," Carrie agreed. "I was telling Emma about it this morning—"

"You started telling me this morning but didn't finish until this afternoon actually," Emma teased Carrie.

"That's because I'm confused," Carrie admitted. "I was so glad to see him that I just wanted to melt, but I had to tell Josh he was coming, and—"

"Wait a second," Sam interrupted. "You mean Josh as in the Josh from your high school who you broke up with? What does he have to do with anything?"

"If you had ever answered any of my letters, you'd know," Carrie said archly. "I stopped writing to you after you didn't answer the first four."

"So sue me, I'm a crummy correspondent," Sam said. She straightened out her legs and mindlessly did some leg stretches as she talked. "Anyway, tell me now."

"He was supposed to go to Stanford, but he changed his mind and decided to go to Yale," Carrie said.

"To be near you?" Sam asked.

"He says that's not the only reason, but yeah, I think so."

"You femme fatale, you," Sam teased. "So go on."

"So I've been kind of seeing him again," Carrie said. "But like I told Emma, I love him, but I'm not *in* love with him."

"Guys hate it when you say that," Sam remarked.

"This guy was no exception," Carrie said.

"Let me get this straight," Sam said. "You were totally hot for Josh and you were sleeping with him in high school. And then you broke up with him, so that ended that.

27

Then by the end of the summer you were with Billy. Now Josh is back in the picture and Billy came to visit, and Josh is not a happy camper. Have I got this right?"

"Right," Carrie agreed. "But Josh and I aren't really going out now. It's not like it was before. We don't spend as much time together and we haven't had sex since we broke up last spring."

"Does he know you're sleeping with Billy?" Sam asked.

"I had to tell him the truth," Carrie said.

"Wow, this is like something on a soap opera," Sam marveled.

"Josh had a fit when I told him Billy was coming up to Yale," Carrie said. "He just went nuts in my dorm room, ranting about how patient he's been, and asking how I could be with Billy when we were seeing each other again."

"He kind of has a point," Emma said gently.

"Hey, she's not engaged, no guy has a claim on her," Sam pointed out. "I say go for the gusto!"

"The thing is, Josh is my best friend. I'm just not seeing him the same way he's seeing me," Carrie explained.

"I told you, Carrie, I think it's kinder if you stop seeing him again and really stick to it this time," Emma said.

"Oh, I just don't know," Carrie moaned. "I really don't."

Sam shook her head and looked at Emma. "If your love life is as hot as Carrie's, I'm going to have a fit."

"Hey, you have Goofy!" Emma teased Sam.

"Goofy is too shy even to try to kiss me," Sam groaned, "much as I might like him to."

"So you kiss him!" Carrie said.

"I'm afraid I'll scare him off," Sam said with a sigh. She threw herself back on the pillows. "Honestly, it's completely humiliating. I'm leading the love life of a nun! It's actually going downhill, and it didn't have very far to slide!"

Emma and Carrie laughed. "I have no doubt you'll make up for it in the future," Carrie said.

"Yeah, well, I'll just have to get my thrills vicariously for a while," Sam decided philosophically. She reached out her foot and nudged Emma in the leg. "You're very quiet, Ms. Cresswell. How's Goucher? Have you heard from Kurt? And speaking of nuns, did you lose *your* virginity yet?"

"Boring, no, and no." Emma laughed. "I wrote to Kurt, but he didn't answer my letter."

"I'm sorry," Sam said.

Emma shrugged. "I'm the one who broke up with him," she reminded her friends. "It was my call, and I still believe I did the right thing. But I can't stop thinking about him," she admitted.

"He loves you, Emma," Carrie said. "I'm sure of that."

"Then why didn't he answer my letter?" Emma asked. When there was no answer from Carrie or Sam, she just sighed. "School is excruciatingly boring, frankly, so it's not like there's anything to take my mind off him."

"Did you send in your application to the Peace Corps?" Sam asked.

"No," Emma admitted, staring down at her lap. "I probably couldn't ever do it. It's just a stupid dream."

Sam jumped up. "God, are we boring or what? Here we are, three incredibly fine babes on vacation, and we're sitting in a hotel room moaning and groaning. Let's go find some fun! Let's go get wild!"

"I thought you had two shows to do," Emma said.

"True," Sam agreed, checking her hair in the mirror over the dresser, "and I've got to get over there. But after that, the sky is the limit! No cute guy in Orlando is safe tonight!" she predicted. "Why, you may ask?"

"Why?" Carrie and Emma asked on cue.

"Because we rule!" Sam crowed. "This is going to be *some* vacation. Am I right or am I right?"

"You're right!" Carrie answered.

"Righter than right!" Emma said.

"Good," Sam said. "One for all and all for one, that's my motto." She checked her watch. "Wow, gotta boogie. Listen, just hop on the monorail in about a half-hour. Ask at the information center for the Rocking Fifties Revue. Here, I got some guest passes for you. You can't miss me. I'll be the incredibly cute redhead dancing in the second row who deserves to get discovered!"

Sam flew toward the door, but stopped suddenly and turned back to her two friends. "I'm just so glad you guys are here, you know?"

The happiness on Carrie's and Emma's faces was the only answer Sam needed.

THREE

Carrie and Emma watched eagerly as the singers and dancers went into the big finale of the Rocking Fifties Revue. It was spectacular, featuring wild jitterbugging, lifts, cartwheels, and incredible singing. At the finish all six girls did handstands that flashed their colorful crinolines, and the guys stood behind them and caught their legs. The singers belted out the final notes of a rock oldie, and the female dancers cartwheeled to their feet and then fell into splits. Carrie and Emma both jumped up, whistling and applauding madly with the rest of the audience.

As the performers scampered offstage, Danny came up to Carrie and Emma. He was dressed in jeans and a polo shirt, and was wearing rimless glasses. He looked absolutely darling, both girls thought.

"Hi," he said in his low voice.

"Well, hi there!" Carrie said. "You're off duty, I see."

Danny nodded. "I try to catch Sam's evening shows. I'm only Goofy during the day."

Emma smiled at him. "She was great up there."

"Wasn't she?" Danny said eagerly. "And she can sing, too, even though she's not very confident about that."

"You're a Sam fan, huh?" Carrie teased him.

Danny blushed. "She's talented," he said, looking down at his loafers.

"I am, aren't I?" Sam said, running over to them. She had thrown on a blue T-shirt and a pair of oversized white shorts held up with a man's necktie. She looked flushed and happy.

Carrie hugged her. "You were so terrific!"

"Did you really think so?" Sam asked. "I almost fell over in that handstand tonight, it was a good thing Trevor grabbed my ankles just in time."

"Trevor loves to grab your ankles," Danny said darkly.

33

"Are you jealous?" Sam asked him hopefully.

Danny shrugged and looked at the ground. "I just know Trevor," he mumbled.

"So are you guys ready to motor?" Sam asked her friends. "The night is young!"

"Would you like to come with us?" Emma asked Danny.

"Oh, no, I, uh . . . I have things to do," Danny said, backing away. "See ya."

"See what I mean?" Sam said with a sigh. "He's hopelessly shy."

"Just give him time," Carrie advised. "He really likes you, and he thinks you're mega-talented. That means a lot."

"Not if I can't even get him to kiss me, it doesn't!" Sam said as they headed for the monorail.

"I love it here," Carrie announced as they climbed on board the high-speed train. "It's total fantasyland!"

Emma smiled. She was having a great time, too. It was funny, but even though she'd traveled to many of the most exciting, jet-set-type places in the world, there was something really special about this place. Maybe it was because she was with her friends, she thought.

"So, here's what I was thinking," Sam said. "There's a great new club in town called Stingray's. There's a hot pink Stingray convertible on the roof and another one inside the club. They play a fantastic mix of music, including a lot of oldies—great dance music—and the cutest guys in town go there. Most of the hoofers, tweeters, and wavers end up there every night."

"Hoofers, tweeters, and wavers?" Carrie asked, completely perplexed.

"Dancers, singers, and the kids who wear the costumes—you know, Mickey, Goofy . . . " Sam translated.

"Cute," Emma said with a laugh.

"So, you guys up for it?" Sam asked.

"Sounds good to me!" Carrie said.

"Me, too," Emma agreed.

A couple of minutes later the three girls had alighted from the monorail and were walking down the hall to their hotel room.

"Whew, I'm pooped," Sam said, throwing herself on one of the beds. "I did four shows earlier today before I met you two at the airport."

"We don't have to go out if you don't want to," Carrie said. "We could wait until tomorrow."

"Are you kidding?" Sam said, sitting up quickly. "Let me just take a shower, and I'll be a new woman. Oh, also, this new woman could use some clothes—or else I have to go back to that prison cell I rent by the month to change."

"Sure, wear anything you want," Emma said, surveying the clothes she'd hung up earlier so she could decide what to wear. "The only problem is, you're five inches taller than I am. A lot of my stuff won't fit you."

"And mine will be too short *and* too baggy," Carrie said, opening a drawer to pull out a forest green T-shirt.

"I'll cope," Sam said, disappearing into the bathroom.

"Hey, the red light is flashing on the phone," Carrie said.

"It means we have a message at the front desk," Emma explained. "Call down and see."

While Carrie called the front desk, Emma held a cute red shorts outfit up to her as she looked in the mirror. She still had a hard time deciding what to wear. Before her summer at Sunset Island, all she'd ever worn were designer originals. Since she'd wanted to fit in with the other kids on the island, one of the first things she'd done when she'd arrived was to shop for a more normal-looking wardrobe at the local trendy boutique. Now she had started to mix and match some of her more expensive items with the newer, funkier ones, trying to create her very own look. Still, she didn't feel nearly as secure about standing out from the crowd as Sam did. For too many years Emma's mother had harped at her about how "those who matter" dress. To Kat Cresswell, "those who matter" were simply those with enough old money. Emma despised her mother's attitude, but it was difficult to escape the years and years of conditioning.

"Really?" Carrie said excitedly into the phone. She grabbed a notepad and a pen and started to scribble something down. At that moment Sam turned the shower on in the bathroom and started singing a song from her revue.

"What's the number again?" Carrie said, trying to hear over the cacophony from the bathroom.

Emma held up a short stonewashed denim

skirt. *Too ordinary*, she decided, and hung it back in the closet.

"My roommate from college called," Carrie told Emma, hanging up the phone. "She left a message that I got a call from Rick Gerabaldi at *Rock On* magazine. He left his home number and said I should call right away."

"*Rock On* is the magazine you sold those photos of Graham Perry to, isn't it?" Emma asked.

Carrie nodded. It was incredible, but true, that Carrie had been fortunate enough to be hired as an au pair for rock superstar Graham Perry's two children. Graham (who was known as Graham Templeton in his private life) and his wife, Claudia, had been very supportive of Carrie's burgeoning career as a photographer, and had suggested that she take some backstage shots at a concert Graham gave on Sunset Island. Because of Graham's support, Carrie had had access to shots that much more experienced photographers would have killed for. She'd sold some to *Rock On*, and they had even sent her to New York to cover a Graham Perry concert at Madison Square Garden.

"I wonder why he left his home number," Carrie mused as she picked up the phone and dialed eight for a long-distance line.

"Maybe it's something wonderful that just couldn't wait until tomorrow," Emma said.

"What couldn't wait until tomorrow?" Sam asked as she opened the bathroom door. She was dripping wet and wrapped in a towel.

"Hello? Is Rick Gerabaldi in?" Carrie asked, holding up a hand to Sam to shush her.

"Rick Gerabaldi, the guy from *Rock On* magazine?" Sam asked.

"The same," Emma confirmed.

"Hello, Rick?" Carrie said. "This is Carrie Alden, returning your call. I hope I'm not calling too late."

Sam grabbed another towel to dry her hair, and both she and Emma listened to Carrie's half of the conversation.

"Yes . . . uh-huh . . . uh-huh . . ." Carrie said. A shocked expression came over her face, and she sat down on the bed. "Really?" she said. Emma and Sam were both watching her avidly. "I . . . well, I'd love to!" Carrie said. "I just need to talk it over with some people first . . . yes, I'll call you right back," Carrie promised. "Oh, and Rick? Thank you!" she said fervently. Rick must have said something to that, because Carrie laughed. "Yes, I'll have to thank him, too!"

Carrie hung up the phone and turned to her two friends, her eyes shining. "You guys are not going to believe this," she said slowly.

"He wants you to be his love slave?" Sam guessed.

"Better," Carrie said. "There's a big Graham Perry concert in Miami tomorrow night. Faith O'Connor—she does the major celebrity interviews for *Rock On*—is supposed to go down and spend the day interviewing Graham for a big lead article for the magazine. The photographer who was supposed to fly down to Miami with Faith broke his leg on his motorcycle this afternoon, so Rick needs to book a new photographer right away. He said that he was on the phone with Graham confirming Faith's interview for tomorrow when he got word about the photographer, so he told Graham. And Graham said to call me because—and I quote—'she's the greatest.' So Rick did!"

"Oh, Carrie, I'm so happy for you!" Emma

said. "And it's just coincidence that you're already in Florida?"

Carrie nodded. "Rick had no idea. He was ready to book me a flight from New Haven." Carrie hugged herself, as if she couldn't quite believe her good luck, and stared off into the distance. "It's going to be a big, major feature. It would be by far the biggest thing I've had a chance to do!" She looked over at Sam and Emma. "The only thing is, I'd have to get on a plane to Miami tomorrow morning, and I really don't want to ruin our plans," Carrie said.

"Oh, come on," Emma said. "You can't possibly pass up this opportunity!"

Carrie looked over at Sam. "Sam?" she asked.

"Carrie, babe, sometimes I worry that that high IQ of yours has made you stupid. There is a very simple solution to all this. Emma and I will go with you!"

"You would?" Carrie asked eagerly. "But what about your job? Do you have an understudy?"

"I only have one more day before I would have been on vacation, anyway," Sam said. "I'll just get sick! Simple!"

"Maybe you shouldn't do that," Emma said. "You could get in trouble."

"Emma, Emma, Emma," Sam chided. "Isn't it a pain in the butt to be perfect all the time?"

Emma blushed. "It's your life," she mumbled.

"Rightamundo!" Sam agreed. "And I'm starting to feel ever so peaked. I might even be unwell upon the morrow," she said dramatically, holding the back of one wrist to her forehead.

Emma laughed. "You, my dear, are the one who is a pain in the butt."

"I know, but at least I'm amusing," Sam said. "And I do come up with the occasional brilliant idea."

"So it's a go?" Carrie asked eagerly. "Emma?"

"It's a great idea," Emma agreed.

"God, this is going to be awesome!" Sam screamed. "Miami at Christmas! Do you know the number of college guys that'll be there on break? I think my love life is about to pick up."

"I have to call Rick back," Carrie said, reaching for the phone. "I'll ask him to phone me with the number of the flight he books me on, and then you can get tickets for the same one."

"Okay, we're going to celebrate tonight," Sam decided, looking through Emma's clothes while Carrie placed her call. "What do you have that will make guys drop to the floor and worship at my feet?"

"I'm afraid my wardrobe will be completely tame to you," Emma said.

Sam held up the denim skirt that Emma had rejected as too ordinary. "Except you forgot one thing," Sam said. "If this skirt is short on you, it will be just about indecent on me. Can I wear it?"

"Be my guest," Emma said.

"Okay, we're all set," Carrie said happily, hanging up the phone.

"Cool," Sam said, zipping herself into Emma's skirt. "How does this look?" she asked, twirling around in a circle.

"Short," Carrie said.

"Very short," Emma added. "I suggest you don't bend over."

"So I'll wear cute panties," Sam said. "What do you have to go with it?"

"Help yourself," Emma said, gesturing to the drawer where she'd neatly folded her tops.

"Hey, can I wear the tapestry vest you had on at the airport?" Sam asked. "Please, pretty please?"

Emma took it off a hanger and handed it to her. Sam donned the vest over her bare skin, buttoning it over her breasts but leaving the lower buttons undone so that her tanned midriff showed.

"Well?" Sam asked.

"I just don't know how you do it," Carrie marveled. "I've never seen anybody do with clothes what you can do with them."

"It's a gift," Sam said, admiring her reflection fore and aft in the mirror. She turned back to Carrie. "How about if I help you two put together killer outfits?"

"I don't know," Carrie said. "I'd feel naked in the kind of clothes you wear."

"Live dangerously," Sam instructed. She went to the other side of the closet, where Carrie's clothes hung, and pawed through them. "This is max!" Sam said, pulling out a long, white, lacy T-shirt.

"It's a beach coverup," Carrie laughed.

"Correction," Sam said. "It *was* a beach coverup. If you wear this white stretch miniskirt and that white stretch aerobics top underneath, it will be sensational." Sam reached for the skirt and the top and handed them to Carrie.

"But—" Carrie protested.

"No buts," Sam interrupted. "Like I said, live dangerously."

Carrie looked undecided for a second. "All right, I will," she said finally. "I'll try it on, anyway. But you two have to promise you'll tell me if I look fat." Carrie headed into the bathroom to change.

"Now, what do we do with little Miss Heiress?" Sam mused, eyeing Emma critically. "Something that will not involve a little black dress and a string of your grandmother's pearls . . ."

"I can dress myself," Emma answered with a slight edge to her voice.

"Hey, I'm only kidding, Em. You know that, don't you?" Sam said anxiously. "I'm just having fun. You can dress however you want."

Emma saw the contrite look on Sam's face and felt guilty for taking the whole thing so seriously. She gave herself a mental shake. That was the old Emma talking, she realized, the one who could freeze people out, just like her mother did. The last thing in the world she wanted was to be anything at all like her mother.

"Sorry," Emma said with a small smile. "Go ahead, experiment."

Sam did. An hour later, when the three girls surveyed themselves in the mirror, they liked what they saw. Emma and Sam had finally convinced Carrie that she looked fabulous in the white outfit. Sam had even gotten some mascara and blush onto Carrie's face, despite the fact that Carrie almost never wore makeup. Emma had on a short pink dress with black lace-trimmed Lycra bike shorts underneath. It was an outfit she never would have put together, not in a million years. Sam still had on Emma's supershort skirt and sexy vest, and she had pouffed out her hair and sprayed it into a mass of wild curls.

"You're absolutely certain that I don't look fat?" Carrie asked, looking down at the bare skin peeking through her lacy T-shirt.

"Carrie, you have a great figure!" Emma assured her. "You look hot."

"We all do," Sam stated. "What do you say we go break a few hearts?"

They got a taxi in front of the hotel and

quickly made it over to Stingray's. The music was so loud that they could hear it before they were even out of the taxi. Carrie glanced up at the car on the roof bathed in a hot pink light as she and Emma followed Sam into the club.

The cavernous room pulsated with the beat of a rap record played at ear-shattering volume. Strobe lights pulsated to the beat of the music, illuminating the gyrating dancers on the huge dance floor. Suspended near the ceiling, over the balcony, was a second Sting-ray convertible, circa 1960, painted candy-apple red. On the balcony a pretty girl dressed in sixties-style clothes dipped a giant wand into a tub of soapy water and blew giant bubbles down on the crowd.

"Sam! Come dance with me!" A short, muscular black guy enveloped Sam in a hug and pulled her toward the dance floor.

"Ed, these are my friends Emma and Carrie. Ed's the dance captain of two of the revues," Sam explained over the deafening music. "That means he's in charge when the choreographer's gone. He's one of the best dancers at the park."

"Nice to meet you," Ed yelled in a friendly fashion, then he tugged Sam onto the dance floor. Sam went willingly, giving Emma and Carrie a little wave over her shoulder.

"Hi there, remember me?" asked a deep male voice from behind Emma. She and Carrie turned around and looked up at a cute, all-American-looking guy who was grinning at them.

Carrie and Emma stared at him blankly.

"Sorry," said Emma. "I think you have me confused with someone else."

"No, I don't," he corrected her. He cleared his throat, put out his hand, smiled like he was in a toothpaste ad, and said, "Thanks, and have a wonderful stay here at the Magic Kingdom!"

"The bellhop from the hotel!" Emma laughed, recognizing him now.

Another guy came up next to him, smiling easily.

"Hey, Kevin, you managed to find the two cutest girls in the place," the other guy said. "What is it, some kind of radar?"

The first guy laughed. "I'm Kevin Carlton," he said, introducing himself to Emma and Carrie. "And this is my not-so-subtle roommate, Jonathan Livitowitz."

Emma and Carrie introduced themselves.

"Do you work at the hotel, too?" Carrie asked Jonathan.

"Part-time," Jonathan said. "I have the world's easiest job. I just hang out in the office reading textbooks and waiting for an accident."

"He's a medical student," Kevin explained. "He works a few nights a week covering for the regular doctor, just in case any guest needs medical care," he explained.

"Well, gee, I feel much safer now," Carrie said, grinning up at Jonathan's sparkling green eyes.

"Dance?" Jonathan asked Carrie.

The record segued into another that featured a bass line so loud Emma could feel her skin vibrate.

"So, do you like your job?" Emma yelled over the music.

"It's okay," Kevin said with a shrug. "I work as a waiter, too. Between the two jobs I'm making enough to put myself through college."

Emma nodded with interest, but actually the image of Kurt jumped into her mind. He, too, was working hard to put himself through school.

"Are you a student?" Kevin asked.

Emma nodded. "Freshman at Goucher," she said.

Kevin raised his eyebrows. "My, my, the most expensive college in the country," he said.

Emma smiled because she didn't know what to say. She hadn't expected him to have heard of tiny, elite Goucher, but evidently he had. Now she was sorry she'd mentioned it.

"I guess you don't have to worry about working two jobs, huh?" Kevin said, taking in Emma's Cartier watch and her large diamond stud earrings.

This is beginning to remind me entirely too much of Kurt, she thought. *Why should I have to defend myself because I'm rich?*

"Listen, I—" Emma began, but she was interrupted by the return of Sam with her friend Ed.

"Whew, it's hot out there!" Sam yelled, holding her hair off her neck with one hand and fanning herself with the other.

"It's great aerobic exercise," Ed yelled. "Let's go dance some more!"

"Oh, Ed, you haven't even worked up a sweat yet," Sam moaned. "You're in better shape than anybody I know. It's disgusting."

"Would you like to dance?" Kevin asked Emma.

"Actually, I was going to suggest we go get some food," Sam said before Emma could respond. "I'm starved. Where's Carrie?"

"I'm right here," Carrie said, coming up to them with Jonathan in tow.

Everyone was introduced all around.

"So, who's hungry?" Sam asked. "We could go next door to Lefty's for pizza."

They all agreed it was a great idea, and started for the door. But before they got there they ran into Danny.

"Danny!" Sam said with surprise. "I can't believe you're here!"

"Hi," he said.

Sam introduced the guys to Danny. "You never go dancing," Sam marveled.

"Well, tonight I just, um, felt like it," Danny said.

"Hey, want to come with us for pizza?" Sam asked. "Or I guess you don't, if you wanted to dance."

"Oh, well, I guess I could dance later," Danny said. He fell in with the group, and they headed next door to Lefty's.

"I just cannot believe it," Sam whispered

to Emma and Carrie when Danny was up ahead talking with Ed, Kevin, and Jonathan. "I've begged him dozens of times to come to Stingray's with me, and he always turns me down! Why did he show up tonight?"

"Because he's obviously crazy about you, and he finally got up the nerve, that's why!" Carrie whispered back.

Sam stopped and stared at her friends. "You think so? You don't think he just wanted to go dancing? I mean, I didn't even tell him that's where we'd be!"

"He guessed!" Emma said as they started walking again. "Like you said, the guy is crazy about you."

"Gee, maybe it's actually true," Sam marveled.

"Sam, you're the one who told us!" Carrie said, laughing.

"Well, sure," Sam said, "but that doesn't mean I really believed it!"

Emma and Carrie were still laughing when they walked into the pizza parlor.

FOUR

"Whoa, did you see that guy?" Sam asked. She turned around to catch another glimpse of the retreating figure in ripped white jeans and a sky-blue T-shirt.

Carrie and Emma spun her back around. "No distractions," Emma warned. "We've got to find our luggage." It was the next afternoon, and the girls had just landed at Miami International Airport.

"This place is a zoo," Carrie remarked as a girl in running shorts darted away from two guys in fraternity sweatshirts with the sleeves cut off.

"I've always wanted to come here for Christmas break," Sam said with glee. "I've heard it's the wildest place on earth. She looked up at the television screen suspended near the rear wall of the baggage pickup area. "It says the luggage from our flight is coming in on carousel 8A."

"Hey, look over there!" Emma said, pointing to a cute guy holding up a sign with Carrie's name on it.

The three girls headed over to him.

"Hi, I'm Carrie."

"Hi, I'm Mark Weiss," the guy said, shaking Carrie's hand. "I'm Faith O'Connor's assistant, from *Rock On* magazine. She asked me to come over and meet your plane."

"Wow, that was really nice of her," Carrie said. She introduced Emma and Sam. "I think our luggage is about to come in."

"Give me the tickets and I'll get it for you," Mark offered.

"You're on," Sam said. All three girls handed Mark their baggage checks.

"I rented a car for you," Mark continued. "I hope a Pontiac Firebird is okay."

"Oh, fine," Carrie said. She looked like she was in a daze.

"Great!" Mark said with a grin. He scanned the baggage pickup area, which was a maze of people. "Listen, it's a mob scene here. Why don't you three just have a seat over there?" he said, pointing to a nearby cluster of chairs and couches, "and after I retrieve your stuff we'll go get your car. Oh, can you describe the bags to me?"

"Let's see," Carrie mused, "Emma's is a white leather case that has her initials in gold, Sam's is a black-and-white tweed, and mine's a green duffle bag." Carrie blushed. "It's um, left over from camp," she explained.

Mark nodded. "See you in a jiffy!"

"I think I need to get new luggage," Carrie muttered.

"It doesn't matter," Emma said kindly.

"Yeah, she can say that because her stuff is carefully encased in white leather designer luggage," Sam snorted.

"I can't believe this is happening!" Carrie said, eager to change the subject. She was all set to have the time of her life, and she was not about to let Sam's silly snipes about Emma's wealth cause any tension between them. "I had no idea someone from the magazine was going to meet me, let alone rent a car for me!"

"Too bad they didn't rent Mark for you," Sam said.

Emma laughed. "Did anyone besides me

ever suggest that you have a one-track mind?"

"He *is* cute," Carrie agreed. She looked over at Mark, standing by the baggage carousel. He was not too tall but well built, his auburn hair just brushed the back of his collar, and his brown eyes radiated a warmth and intelligence that Carrie found really appealing.

"Ooh, serious hot flash when he bent over to pick up your suitcase," Sam said, nudging Carrie in the ribs and pointing to Mark's buns.

"She's hopeless!" Emma decided.

Mark had their suitcases loaded on a cart, which the skycap wheeled over to them. "Okay, I'll just run out and bring the car around, and we'll be off," he said.

"I've got to remember to call my parents when we get to the hotel," Sam said, slipping on some sunglasses. "I sort of told them I might come home in a few days, so that I'd be there for Christmas day and New Year's."

"Did you ever have any intention of doing that?" Emma asked with surprise.

"Not really," Sam admitted. "They just were driving me nuts on the phone."

"My parents were disappointed that I wouldn't be home for Christmas, either," Carrie said. "I just wish I could be two places at once. We've always had the greatest times, decorating the tree, singing carols—and my dad makes his world-famous eggnog," she reminisced wistfully.

Emma attempted a smile, but it didn't work. She really couldn't relate to the idea of warm, loving parents who cared if she was around for a holiday. Her parents had been embroiled in a messy divorce for almost two years. As soon as it became final, her father was planning to marry a twenty-three-year-old girl Emma had never even met. And her mother was no better. A totally self-involved woman, desperate to stay young, she had recently become engaged to a twenty-four-year-old artist named Austin Payne. Even after Emma's mother had found out that Austin was cheating on her, she'd made excuses for him and taken him back. It seemed like both her parents were intent on finding partners closer to their daughter's age than to their own. Emma found it horribly embarrassing.

Neither parent had ever stayed in Boston for Christmas. When Emma was a child, she'd simply jetted off with them to which-ever playground of the rich and famous they were headed for that year. But now that she was grown up, she wasn't about to follow either of them to St. Moritz or the French Riviera.

"You're so lucky, Emma," Sam said.

"What?" Emma asked, startled back from her thoughts.

"That you don't have to report in to Mommy and Daddy like some total child," Sam said with a sigh. "I cannot imagine being both rich and free. It must be heaven."

"Okay, ready when you are," Mark said, coming up to them quickly.

They headed out into the bright sunshine and got into the gleaming white car parked at the curb.

"Did you want to drive?" Mark asked Carrie before he got in. "I mean, it is your car."

"Yeah, but I have no idea where I'm going," Carrie laughed, getting in the passenger side.

They quickly got on to the freeway. As they got off the freeway and drove towards the beach front, stores and apartment buildings gave way to elegant hotels. When Mark turned the car onto the strip of property that lined Miami Beach, the hotels were the most luxurious and impressive of all.

"Regency Beach," Sam read, ogling the limos that lined the circular drive leading to their hotel.

The Regency Beach was the most famous of the famous hotels on Miami Beach. Everyone from Madonna to Bob Hope had stayed there. Huge white marble pillars stood in front of the building, each illuminated by colored lights reflecting from one of four fountains. Crushed glass enmeshed in the white stone of the hotel caught the sunlight and glistened like tiny diamonds.

The members of the staff were dressed in pristine white tuxedos with the Regency Beach logo embroidered in peacock blue on their left shoulder. Sam noted how cute the girls looked in their white tuxedo uniforms and made a mental note to get one some time.

"Pinch me, I'm dreaming," Sam said as they walked into the lobby. The lobby itself reversed the color scheme, with a lush peacock blue carpet laid over gleaming white marble floors.

"Since Graham and his band are staying here, we thought this would be the most convenient place for you to stay, too," Mark explained.

They registered quickly and headed up to their room, a bellhop following them with their luggage.

"Oh wow, you can see the ocean from here!" Sam screamed, racing to the window as soon as she got into the room.

"This okay?" Mark asked the girls as he handed the bellhop a tip.

"This is . . . unbelievable," Carrie breathed.

The corner room had sliding glass doors that opened onto a balcony overlooking the ocean. The large room accommodated two double beds, a luxurious dressing table and a separate area containing a sofa and table, several chairs, a bar and a refrigerator.

Carrie noticed a large basket of fruit wrapped in red cellophane on the dresser. She read the tiny card that was attached: *Thanks for coming to my rescue. Rick.*

"He didn't have to do that," Carrie said to Mark. "I feel like I'm the one who should be thanking him for the assignment."

Mark grinned. "He doesn't do it for everyone," he said. "He must think a lot of your photography."

"I'm not kidding, I could do a swan dive to the ocean from here!" Sam called from the patio. "You guys have to see this!"

"So here's the schedule," Mark told Carrie. "Faith will meet you in the lobby at one o'clock so you two can spend a couple of hours with Graham just hanging out, talking, taking pictures in his room. He's already okayed that. Then *Rock On* is giving a cocktail party for Graham at five o'clock in the penthouse suite—you can bring your friends to that. The concert starts tonight at ten, and that's about it," he concluded. "You cool with all that?"

"Sounds great," Carrie agreed.

"Okay, well, if you need anything, I'm in room eleven-eighty-two," Mark said, flashing his terrific grin. "Hey, nice to meet you!" he called to Sam and Emma, who were leaning on the balcony railing with their faces tilted up to the sun.

"Can you believe all this?" Carrie asked her friends as she joined them out on the balcony.

"I thought Sunset Island was guy-watching paradise," Sam said, "but that was

61

before I saw Miami. Just look down there. It's a guy smorgasboard!"

"Well, you two can go enjoy it," Carrie said. "I have to go meet Faith in the lobby in twenty minutes, then we're going to Graham's room. I can't wait to see him again!"

"Hey, that girl is wearing one of those thong bikinis," Sam said, pointing down to a tiny figure in hot pink. "Wow, you can see her entire butt!"

All three girls leaned over to see.

"I think it's gross," Emma said, wrinkling her perfect nose.

"Is it legal?" Carrie wondered.

"Spoilsports!" Sam scoffed. "Just for that I think I'll buy one!"

Carrie laughed. "Well, if you don't get arrested, I'll meet you guys back here later this afternoon. There's a cocktail party at five that you're invited to," Carrie said. "I'm going to change and go."

"And we're going to go break a few hearts," Sam said to Emma. "Hey, I'll wear my white bikini if you'll wear your black suit with the mesh," Sam said.

Emma had never worn the black bathing suit with the mesh inserts that she'd bought during the summer. She'd modeled it for her friends when she'd first gotten it, but that was all. It just didn't seem like her. Still, she'd brought it with her, so maybe she really wanted to wear it after all, she thought.

"You're on," Emma promised.

Carrie rushed out the door with her two cameras around her neck, and Emma and Sam changed into their bathing suits.

"I don't know about this," Emma said, surveying her image in the mirror.

"It's great," Sam said. "There's something about that ice-princess look of yours wrapped in a slutty swimsuit that will drive guys wild."

"I look slutty?" Emma asked, totally horrified.

"No, no, the suit looks slutty, not you," Sam corrected her, applying some waterproof mascara to her eyelashes.

"I'm changing to the white one," Emma decided, pulling it off.

"Suit yourself," Sam said with a shrug. "No one can force you to take chances."

Emma stopped undressing, her suit halfway to her knees. "I guess I don't take a lot of chances, do I?" she said thoughtfully.

Sam gave her a meaningful look.

"Okay, I'll wear it," Emma decided, pulling the suit back up.

They threw T-shirts and shorts over their suits, packed beach bags, and headed out the door.

"Do we hit the pool or the ocean first?" Sam mused.

"I vote for the ocean," Emma said. "It's much more romantic."

"Sure," Sam agreed. "Oh, and remind me we have to cruise the shops later to find me one of those thong suits."

"Would you really wear that?" Emma asked as they rode the elevator down to the lobby.

"But of course," Sam said. "Hey, you're only young with perfecto buns once, you know?"

"Yes, but do you want the whole world to see those buns?" Emma said as they crossed the lobby. Donning sunglasses as they headed out into the bright sunshine, Sam replied breezily, "Oh, sure. My only question is, how much sunscreen do you have to use on body parts that have never seen any sun before?"

FIVE

Faith O'Connor was waiting in the lobby when Carrie arrived.

"I hope I'm not late," Carrie said after she introduced herself.

"You're right on time," Faith assured her as they walked toward the elevator. "It was great that you could fill in at the last minute," she added.

"I'm just so excited to get the assignment," Carrie admitted.

The elevator came and they got on.

"This is planned as a very major profile," Faith explained, "really in-depth. I met with Graham once already out at his home on Sunset Island. Ever hear of the place?"

"Um, I think so," Carrie said. She wasn't sure why, but she didn't want to tell Faith that she had worked for Graham and Claudia on the island taking care of their kids. Maybe it was because she thought it sounded so juvenile—who would take seriously a photographer who had recently been a babysitter?

"So the plan is that I'll just talk with him, and you can unobtrusively snap away," Faith said. "My guess is he'll be more comfortable with you there, since you've shot him before," Faith said.

"I hope so," Carrie said, nervously fiddling with the strap on one of her cameras.

"You'll be fine," Faith said, giving Carrie a warm smile. "I thought the shots you took of him before were terrific."

Carrie smiled back gratefully and studied Faith O'Connor. Faith was about Carrie's height, but very slim and fine-boned. She looked to be in her early thirties. Her short, tousled honey-blond hair was streaked lighter in the front, and her clear green eyes were subtly made up with brown eyeliner and mascara. She wore jeans and an embroidered white cotton shirt. The leather belt she sported had a huge turquoise stone over the buckle. Turquoise leather cowboy boots completed the ensemble. The whole effect was casual and professional at the same time. Next to her Carrie felt very young and completely lacking in style. She'd thrown on baggy tan shorts and a blue chambray shirt, and had tied her hair back in a ponytail.

"Okay, you ready?" Faith asked as they stood in front of the door to Graham's suite.

"Sure," Carrie said gamely. She reminded herself that she belonged there, that she really did know Graham, that she was a professional.

"Carrie!" Claudia cried as she opened the door. It was Graham's wife, twenty-five-year-old Claudia Templeton. She looked absolutely thrilled to see Carrie.

"Hi," Carrie said shyly, but Claudia enveloped her in a bear hug. "What a nice surprise! I had no idea you were the photographer for this!"

"I did," Graham said, coming up behind his wife. He was as mesmerizing-looking as ever. Even though he was in his late thirties by now, and had been a rock legend for nearly twenty years, he still radiated a charisma and sex appeal that had women of all ages fantasizing about him. It still amazed Carrie that she had actually worked for—and lived in the same house as—the superstar who stood before her.

"Hi, Graham," Carrie said with a small smile. "Thanks for recommending me for this job."

Claudia swatted Graham playfully. "You knew Carrie was coming and you didn't tell me!"

"It was a surprise," Graham said.

As they all went to sit down Faith shot a look at Carrie. Carrie felt herself wince. She could almost feel the wheels turning inside the reporter's head, trying to place how Carrie fit in with the superstar and his wife. *Photographer, not babysitter*, Carrie reminded herself.

"Wait till I tell the kids I saw you," Claudia said as she sat down next to Graham in a small grouping of comfortable-looking leather chairs. "Oh, can I order anybody anything?" she asked. "Soft drinks? Real drinks?"

"A Diet Coke would be great," Faith said.

"Me, too," Carrie said with a smile. It seemed very strange to be giving Claudia a beverage order, instead of having Claudia give it to her.

"I'll have a scotch and water," Graham called out to Claudia as she went to pick up the phone.

"Graham," she said warningly.

"Just kidding," Graham said with a grin. He looked at Faith and Carrie. "My wife thinks one drink means certain death and destruction."

"Really?" said Faith, casually getting out her notepad. She knew juicy info when it fell into her lap. Years ago Graham had been both an alcoholic and a cocaine addict, but he'd been completely clean and sober for years now. In fact, he was well known for the antidrinking and antidrug rock videos he made as a public service.

"I'm not drinking, if that's the question your poised pen means you're about to ask," Graham said, raising his eyebrows coolly at Faith. "It was a joke."

"Okay," she said easily.

Carrie took the lens caps off her cameras and wandered around the room. She couldn't help but wonder why Graham had even brought it up if he really wasn't drinking.

"I hope you ordered me a double," Graham said after Claudia had hung up.

"Oh, Graham," Claudia sighed. "He's kidding," she said to Faith. "I hope you know he's kidding."

"Sure," Faith said easily. It wasn't apparent what she really thought.

"I'm going into the bedroom to call the kids," Claudia said. "Maybe if you're not too busy you can say hello, Carrie."

Faith shot Carrie another look, but Carrie just busied herself with her camera.

"I'd like to ask you about 'Dream to Die By,'" Faith asked Graham. "Dream to Die By" was a song on Graham's new album. "I listened to it over and over last night. It's very dark."

"Very," Graham agreed.

"It seems to be about self-destruction," Faith said. "Is it your own you're talking about?"

Graham stared pensively out the window, as if he could see all the way to wherever the endless ocean led. Carrie snapped off some photos. "Could be, I suppose," Graham agreed, "but it's not."

"Who then?" Faith pressed.

"Anyone's, everyone's," Graham said evasively.

"Your first wife?" Faith asked.

Everyone knew that Graham's first wife had died of a drug overdose. Shortly after that Graham had gone to the Betty Ford Center to kick those habits himself.

Graham shrugged. "Who knows, who knows?" he said.

"But you did write it on the tenth anniversary of her death," Faith prompted Graham.

Graham smiled at her sardonically. "Well, I see we've done our research."

Carrie moved unobtrusively to the side of the room and clicked away at Graham, catching him with his face turned pensively to the ocean. He had never been like this on Sunset Island. Sometimes he'd gotten mad, and he had a pretty volatile temper, but she'd never seen him morose before.

The interview continued and Carrie kept snapping photos, but in her opinion it really didn't seem to be going well. Graham seemed terribly depressed.

"Graham? Chloe's on the phone. She wants to say hello," Claudia said from the doorway to the bedroom.

Graham excused himself and went into the bedroom.

"Not a happy guy," Faith murmured.

"He's not usually like this," Carrie felt compelled to explain. "He's just . . . I don't know, in a bad mood or something."

Faith raised her eyebrows at Carrie. "How is it you happen to know so much about him?"

"I . . . I took shots of him before, you know that," Carrie said.

Faith and Carrie could hear the couple's voices from the bedroom, but couldn't make out what they were saying. It sounded like they were arguing about something.

"Maybe we should come back later," Carrie suggested.

Faith looked at her like she was out of her mind. "Are you kidding? We may be getting a great scoop here. It's not nearly as interesting if everything is all sweetness and light."

"Graham, no," they heard Claudia say.

Soon Graham came out of the bedroom.

"Sorry," he said, briskly slipping into the chair. "So, ask away!"

"We were talking about 'Dream to Die By,'" Faith reminded him.

"Right," Graham said. He seemed much

more alert now, and completely focused on the interview. "Well, it was a way to deal with demons, past and present," he began.

Carrie could hardly believe it. It was as if a different person had come out of the bedroom. Graham was eloquent, charming, and full of energy and intensity—everything you would expect from a superstar.

Claudia got the door when room service arrived, but Graham was deep into his conversation and barely noticed. Claudia just left them their drinks and went back into the bedroom, shutting the door quietly.

Carrie kept moving to different angles in the room, snapping shots of Graham. He was animated now, leaning forward in his chair to make a point, laughing at himself in a charmingly self-effacing fashion. Even as she concentrated on getting the angles and the lighting right, a thought kept coming back into her mind.

Graham really *was* drinking again.

That's what he had been doing in the bedroom.

And Faith had guessed, too, and would undoubtedly put it in her article.

Halfway through the interview Graham

excused himself, saying he was going to the bathroom. When he came back he was even more animated than before.

Carrie shot two rolls of film, and Faith finally said she had enough for the moment.

"You were great. I really appreciate your being so open with me," Faith said, tucking her pen into her purse.

"My pleasure," Graham said.

Claudia came out of the bedroom and said good-bye with a pinched smile on her face. She hugged Carrie and said she'd see her at the cocktail party in a couple of hours. Something was definitely wrong.

Carrie looked at Faith's face as they waited for the elevator. Was it her imagination, or was Faith wearing a smug look, the look of someone who was about to write something terrible about a superstar? Carrie desperately wanted to prevent that, but she had no idea how to do it.

"Graham seemed . . . in a strange mood," Carrie said, trying to feel Faith out.

"You can say that again," Faith laughed, getting on the elevator.

Carrie bit her lower lip. "Look, I know it's none of my business, but maybe it's not a good idea for you to write that Graham might be . . . having certain problems with, uh, with alcohol," she stammered.

Faith looked surprised. "Is that what you think? That he fell off the wagon?"

Carrie blushed. This was horrible. Maybe Faith hadn't noticed anything, in which case she might have just made the situation much worse. Or maybe she had noticed, and thought Carrie unprofessional to suggest that she omit such telling information in an exposé.

"No, no, I didn't think that," Carrie said hastily.

"Because it's not that," Faith continued. The elevator arrived at Carrie's floor. "It's definitely coke," Faith said.

The elevator door opened. Still Carrie stood there, rooted to the spot.

"Coke, like cocaine?" she asked, completely shocked.

The door closed and they traveled down toward the eighth floor, where Faith's suite was located.

Faith laughed. "You really are young," she said. "Yes, cocaine. I think Graham was snorting up a few lines back there. Now wouldn't America love to know about that?"

The elevator door opened and Faith moved briskly out into the hall.

"See you at the cocktail party later!" Faith called as the door closed on Carrie.

Carrie traveled back up to the eleventh floor in a state of shock. Could it possibly be true? Graham Perry was so vehemently against drugs—he'd done all those antidrug videos and public service announcements. Could he really be snorting cocaine in the middle of an interview?

And was Faith O'Connor about to ruin him completely?

"Look at this bathing suit! Can you believe this?" Sam shrieked when Carrie came into the room. "Is it totally indecent or is it totally indecent?" Sam pranced over in a thong bathing suit in peacock blue.

Carrie looked at her from behind. "It looks like it hurts," Carrie said. "And it has no back."

"I know. It's completely decadent," Sam agreed happily, checking out her reflection.

"So how did it go?" Emma asked Carrie.

"Okay, I guess," Carrie said. She wasn't

ready to talk about her conversation with Faith yet.

"You look upset, though," Emma noted.

"No, I'm just tired," Carrie said. "I think maybe I'll lie down for a few minutes before I get dressed for the cocktail party." Carrie kicked off her shoes and lay down on one of the beds. "Did you guys have fun?"

"Sam found that bathing suit in a clothing shop a few doors down from the hotel," Emma said, "and she wore it out of the store. I don't know if *fun* is the word I would use to describe what followed."

"Oh, come on," Sam chided, plopping down on one of the beds, "it was a riot!"

"Correction—you nearly *caused* a riot," Emma said. "Men of all ages followed us from the store to the beach, to the concession stand, everywhere we went. Frankly, it was embarrassing."

"Hey, I didn't make a date with a single one of them, did I?" Sam pointed out. She lay down on the bed, checking underneath one thin strap of her bathing suit for a tan line. "Hmmm, pretty good," she decided. "So, Carrie, what do I wear to the cocktail party?"

"Something that won't get you arrested,"

Emma suggested as she headed into the bathroom to take a shower.

Carrie shut her eyes. She wasn't interested in listening to Sam and Emma banter. She was really concerned about Graham, and about what Faith might say about him in her article. *Maybe I should talk privately to Claudia . . .*

"Hey, Carrie, wake up!" Sam was shaking her gently.

"Huh? What?" Carrie asked foggily. Then she noticed that Sam and Emma were already dressed, and she bolted upright. "Oh God, how long did I sleep?"

"You're okay," Emma assured her. "You've got a half-hour yet. We got ready early."

"We were nervous," Sam confessed. "Do we look okay?"

Carrie shook her head to clear it and tried to focus on her friends. Emma wore a plain but extremely expensive-looking white off-the-shoulder dress, a single strand of pearls, and flat white sandals. Sam had on her new pink supershort miniskirt with matching suspenders over her neon-orange bra top, and of course her trademark red cowboy boots. Emma's blond hair was blunt-cut into a perfect, shining bob and Sam's hair was sprayed into a mass of wild red curls. Even in Carrie's semiawake state, she had to smile at how totally different they were.

"You both look great," Carrie said. "I'd better jump in the shower. And you guys have to help me—I have no idea what to wear!"

Emma and Sam helped Carrie decide on a simple long chiffon skirt in gold and white with a scoop-necked white sleeveless linen blouse that showed off her great bustline.

"Let me put just a little makeup on you," Sam begged.

"It makes me feel like a clown," Carrie said, making a face. She grabbed her two cameras and some extra film from the dresser.

"Well, at least you're wearing clothes that actually fit now," Sam grumbled as they walked to the elevator. She hated to be thwarted in any of her grand schemes.

"So, who is going to be at this cocktail party again?" Emma asked. It was funny that she felt nervous. After all, she'd entertained and been entertained by the world's most powerful people her entire life. She'd even been presented to the Queen of

England. But somehow a cocktail party for a rock superstar made her as nervous as if she'd never been anywhere.

"Faith and Mark, I guess, and Graham and all of his band, and their wives and girlfriends," Carrie said as the girls got on the elevator. "Beyond that, I don't know."

The party had already begun when the girls entered the large suite. Thirty or forty people were drinking champagne and eating food from a huge buffet spread on a long corner table. Graham's latest CD blared through an excellent sound system someone had set up.

"Wow," Sam breathed when they entered the room. She turned quickly to Emma. "I really look okay?"

Emma smiled reassuringly at Sam. It was amazing that someone as gorgeous and ostentatious as Sam could sometimes be so insecure. "Fabulous," Emma told her.

"I'm going to get some great shots here," Carrie said, lifting one camera and looking around eagerly.

"Hi!" Mark called to them, quickly crossing the room to the three girls. "You look great," he added to Carrie. "Can I get any of you a drink?"

"A Diet Coke or something," Carrie said. Sam and Emma seconded that.

"Be right back," Mark promised, loping away.

Sam nudged Carrie meaningfully. "He's desperate for you," she said.

"Yeah, right," Carrie said, laughing. She lifted her camera and quickly shot Graham in conversation with his bass player near the buffet table.

"I'm telling you, I know desperate when I see—" Sam stopped in midsentence. "That can't be who I think it is," she said, peering across the room at a blond-haired guy in the corner. At that moment the two girls who were partially blocking Sam's view moved, and she grabbed Emma's arm like a vise. "It is! It's Johnny Angel! Omigod, I'm dying."

Emma and Carrie looked across the room. It really *was* Johnny Angel. John Angles, who had changed his name to Johnny Angel after an old rock ballad, was without a doubt the hottest up-and-coming new star in the rock world. His handsome face and lean, muscular body were driving girls wild at his concerts. He had started out as a dancer, and now incorporated athletic, sexy dancing into his act as no male rock star had ever done before. The press was calling him the male Madonna, and comparing his dancing to Paula Abdul's. The amazing thing was that Johnny Angel was only twenty-six years old, and his first album had only been out for four months. At that very moment his first single, "Breathless for You," was number one on the rock charts.

"Maybe Johnny's a friend of Graham's," Carrie said.

"They just met, actually," Mark said, handing the girls their drinks. "He's opening for Graham tonight, so we thought we'd invite him and his band to the cocktail party."

"Is he married?" Sam said, staring across the room.

"Not that I know of," Mark said.

"Engaged? Promised? Here with anyone?" Sam asked.

"All I can vouch for is that he came to this party by himself," Mark said with a laugh. "Beyond that, you're on your own."

"I'm going to get him," Sam said, her eyes narrowing.

"Sam!" Emma said, shocked at her friend's behavior.

Sam coolly handed Emma her soda. "Watch me," she said. "Just watch me."

Emma, Carrie, and Mark watched as Sam headed across the room toward Johnny Angel.

SIX

"Oh, excuse me!" Sam said as she bumped into Johnny Angel and sent his glass of champagne flying.

"No, it was my fault," Johnny said, catching Sam's arms and helping to steady her.

"It's kind of crowded in here," Sam said with a sexy grin. She looked ruefully at his now-damp white T-shirt.

"No damage," Johnny said easily. He looked Sam over with curiosity.

"Well, sorry again," Sam said, and began to walk away.

"Wait a second," Johnny said. "I didn't catch your name."

"I didn't throw it," Sam said innocently, and tossed her hair over her shoulder as she walked back to her friends.

"What did you say to him?" Carrie asked

her. "His eyes followed you all the way across the room!"

"It's what I didn't say," Sam said with a grin. "I pretended to bump into him, and then acted totally disinterested. I even pretended not to recognize him. I figure since girls are always throwing themselves at him, that ought to drive him crazy!"

"It's kind of manipulative, isn't it?" Emma asked.

"What difference does it make, as long as it works?" Sam asked her.

"Hey, Carrie! Hi, girls!" Graham ambled over to them and draped an arm around Carrie's shoulder. "I didn't know you two were here with Carrie! It's great to see you!"

"I invited them to the cocktail party," Mark said. "I hope that was all right."

"It's great! No problem!" Graham replied. "I know these girls from the island—great kids, all three of them. So, did you get some good shots this afternoon, Carrie?"

"I think so," Carrie said. She didn't like this at all. Graham really was acting weird. He'd always been very nice to her, but theirs had still been an employer-employee relationship.

"Hello, Graham. I hope you're enjoying the party," Faith said, coming up next to Graham.

"*Rock On* knows how to throw a party," Graham said. "The guys are all having a great time."

"How many more stops do you have on this tour?" Faith asked.

"Twelve or thirteen," Graham said. "I lose track."

"It must be hard on the kids, since Claudia came with you this time out," Faith said sympathetically.

"My kids are fine," Graham said tersely. "Excuse me." He headed for the bathroom. Faith didn't take her eyes off him.

"He's under a lot of pressure," Carrie said softly.

"It's more than that and you know it," Faith said under her breath. She turned to Carrie. "Snap his picture right when he's coming out of the john."

Carrie was taken aback. "What . . . what are you talking about? I mean—"

"Just do what I say," Faith told her. "We might even catch him with a trace of white powder under that gorgeous nose of his."

Carrie looked at her friends, then at

Mark, for help. All three were speechless. She'd have to handle it herself. "Listen, Faith," Carrie began, "I think that's an invasion of privacy or something."

Faith sipped the last of her champagne and eyed Carrie coolly. "Rule number one, Carrie," Faith said, counting on her fingers. "Stars have no privacy. Rule number two," she continued, "you are employed by *Rock On*, get it? I don't know what kind of relationship you have with Graham—although it appears to be pretty personal—but right now you work for me. Now go get the shot."

Carrie bit her lip and walked over to the bathroom, standing a few feet away from the door. Her hands were sweaty and trembling. Before she could lift the camera to her eye, Claudia came flying over to her.

"Hi, Carrie! I told Chloe you were here and she really wanted to say hello this afternoon," Claudia began nervously. Chloe was Claudia and Graham's four-year-old daughter. "I just didn't want to interrupt you while you were working." Claudia's eyes kept darting to the bathroom. It was obvious to Carrie that Claudia knew Graham was in there, and that she did not want his picture snapped when he came out.

At that moment the bathroom door opened and Graham bounded out, sniffing audibly and pinching his nostrils nervously.

Claudia got more animated, even spinning Carrie half around to turn her away from Graham. But Carrie had seen what she'd seen. Even though she didn't actually know anybody who did cocaine, she'd certainly read enough to know the telltale signs. Still, there was no proof, and she absolutely did not want to see Graham's image wrecked this way. Obviously Faith disagreed, though; Carrie could feel the journalist glaring at her from across the room because Carrie hadn't taken the shot she had demanded.

"Mark, conference," Faith said tersely to her assistant. "Excuse us," she added as she and Mark walked briskly away from Sam and Emma.

"What a barracuda," Emma shuddered.

"Yeah, but she dresses great," Sam said. She was still watching Johnny out of the corner of her eye. Across the room he was eyeing her, too. Sam made sure he never saw her looking in his direction.

"What was that whole thing about Carrie taking a picture of Graham coming out of the bathroom?" Emma asked Sam.

"I'm not sure," Sam said. "Something is very weird. It sounded like Faith was insinuating that Graham's coked up, and she wanted Carrie to get a picture of it."

"But that doesn't make any sense!" Emma cried. "Graham is head of Rockers Against Drugs, isn't he? He did that music video and all those TV commercials. . . ."

"Could be he's in trouble," Sam said. She looked across the room at Carrie, who was still having a conversation with Claudia.

Emma shook her head sadly. She'd seen too many very rich and very bored kids her own age experiment with cocaine and get hooked on it. People in her crowd had the money to support such an expensive drug habit, but that didn't stop it from ruining their lives.

"Carrie really looks miserable over there," Emma observed softly. "I think she's—"

"Hey, don't look now, but Mr. Tall, Blond, and Irresistible is heading our way," Sam hissed under her breath.

"I brought you both more champagne," Johnny Angel said, coming up next to Sam and Emma.

"Thanks," both girls said, accepting the crystal fluted glasses.

"So, are you girls with Graham's band?" Johnny asked.

"Not really," Sam said coolly.

"But you do have names," he coaxed with a laugh.

"Emma Cresswell," Emma said.

"Sam Bridges," Sam said.

"And I'm Johnny Angel," Johnny said.

Silence. He was obviously waiting for the usual big reaction.

Sam furrowed her brow and looked at Emma. "Wasn't there some ancient rock song called 'Johnny Angel'? I think I heard it once at an oldies party."

"Could be," Emma said, playing along. She looked at Johnny curiously. "Did your parents name you after a song, or is it coincidence?"

The smile on Johnny's face faltered for a second. "You're kidding, right?"

"About what?" Sam asked.

"I'm Johnny Angel. You know, 'Breathless for You'? That's me. I'm opening for Graham tonight."

Sam shrugged. "I listen mostly to reggae."

"And I spend a lot of time in Europe," Emma added.

Johnny was at a loss for words. Then he threw his head back and laughed. He looked at Sam, his eyes dancing.

"So listen, are you planning to come to the show tonight, or are you going to be tied up with some Rastafarians?"

"I'll be there," Sam said casually. "I'm a friend of Graham's."

"How close a friend?" Johnny asked, raising an eyebrow.

"Graham is married," Sam said demurely. "I'm also a friend of Claudia's."

"So you two already have backstage passes, then," Johnny said.

"Right," Sam agreed.

"Well, then, let's see if when I sing 'Breathless for You,' I can't ignite some kind of fire under that cool exterior of yours."

"I usually wait in Graham's dressing room during the opening act," Sam said.

Johnny's jaw dropped open. Emma had to bite her lip to keep from laughing.

"But tonight I might make an exception," Sam added.

"Great," Johnny managed.

"Well, we have to run," Sam said, handing her empty champagne flute to a passing waiter. "Nice to meet you," she added.

Emma offered her good-byes as Sam half dragged her toward the door and out of the suite.

"Now what did you do that for?" Emma demanded. "I didn't want to leave!"

"Did you see how perfectly that worked?" Sam shrieked, falling against the wall. "Am I a genius or what?"

"Sam!" Emma called impatiently, her hands on her hips.

Sam whirled around and grabbed Emma's wrists with excitement. "He's crazy for me now! Everything went absolutely perfectly! Yes!"

Emma shook Sam loose. "Look, I admit it was masterful manipulation, if you're into such things, but—"

"He is the hottest guy I have ever seen in my life!" Sam rhapsodized, ignoring Emma. "This could be *it*, Em. This could be the guy I've been waiting for my whole life."

"Oh, sometimes you make me so mad I could just smack you!" Emma screamed.

Sam looked at her innocently. "What? What did I do?"

Emma sighed and shook her head. "With the possible exception of my mother, you are the most egocentric person I've ever met.

Did it ever occur to you to think that I might not have wanted to leave? What am I, just an extra to add background color to your life?"

Sam looked stricken. "You're right. Oh, I'm sorry, Em. I wasn't thinking. It's just . . . I was on a roll. I knew that if I seemed so totally disinterested that I'd leave the party rather than stay and talk with him, he'd really believe that I was hard to get!"

"Well, just terrific. Now we're stuck out here in the hall," Emma fumed.

"I guess you could go back in if you wanted to," Sam said in a small voice.

"Forget it," Emma snapped.

"How about if we go up to our room and order room service then?" Sam suggested brightly. "I'm starved! And we can hang out until it's time to go to the concert."

"Fine," Emma said, marching toward the bank of elevators.

"You're really mad at me," Sam said tentatively.

Emma didn't answer her, and they rode in silence up to their room.

"I'll pay for the room service," Sam offered meekly.

"You don't have to do that," Emma said.

"Then what can I do to make you not be mad at me anymore?" Sam pleaded.

At first Emma didn't say anything. Then she started thinking about the performance Sam had just put on. "'I usually wait in Graham's dressing room during the opening act,'" Emma repeated. She burst out laughing. "Where do you get the nerve?"

"I don't know! I think I was just born with it," Sam said with a huge grin on her face. She plopped down on the bed and grabbed the room service menu. "Whoa, check out these prices." She winced. "A grilled cheese sandwich is six dollars!"

The door opened and Carrie came bursting into the room. She sat down heavily on the opposite bed. "What am I going to do?" she moaned.

"What happened?" Emma asked, sitting down next to her.

"Faith thinks Graham is doing coke," Carrie said. "I have to admit, it looks like she's right. She wants me to follow him around to try and get some damning photos. It's like all of a sudden I'm working for the *National Enquirer!*"

"Maybe you should just ask Graham about it yourself," Emma suggested tentatively.

"How can I?" Carrie asked. "I'm here working for *Rock On*. They're the ones who are paying me. But if it hadn't been for Graham, I wouldn't even have the job! God, this is a complete mess!"

"Well, it seems to me it's your job to take the shots," Sam said. "If Graham is doing coke, it's his own responsibility. He could have canceled the interview. It's his problem, not yours."

Emma raised her eyebrows at Sam. "Are things really so simple for you, so cut and dried?"

Sam shrugged. "Why not? What's the big deal?"

"The big deal," Emma began evenly, "is that if Graham is addicted to coke, he can't help himself any more than an active alcoholic can. The big deal is that he needs people who will try to help, not people who will exploit the situation."

"I just don't know what to do," Carrie moaned, fiddling with her camera strap. "I told Faith I had to run up here and get some more film, but I've got to go back and face her."

"If taking that kind of picture goes against your ethics, then don't do it," Emma recommended.

"Emma, no offense, but rich people always seems to find it easy to have this holier-than-thou kind of attitude," Sam said.

"I am not 'rich people' any more than you are 'poor people,'" Emma pronounced icily.

"Okay, sorry," Sam conceded. "But think about Carrie for a minute here. She doesn't have a trust fund to fall back on. Her career is just beginning. This is the work she really wants to do. But she'd probably never get hired again by *Rock On*, or any other magazine, if she doesn't take the shots Faith tells her to take. I'm sure Faith would ruin Carrie's reputation in nothing flat."

"You think she'd do that?" Carrie asked, a horrified look crossing her face.

"Yep," Sam answered matter-of-factly. "She'll say you're uncooperative, unreliable . . ."

"Oh, God," Carrie groaned. "I'm completely screwed on this."

"Look, how about if you keep snapping shots, but you just keep missing the exploitative ones that Faith wants?" Emma suggested.

"I guess that's what I have to try to do," Carrie said. She rose reluctantly from the bed. "This is going to be a very long evening."

"Hang in there," Emma coaxed her.

"Yeah," Sam said. "We'll help any way we can. Just don't jeopardize your career because Graham Perry doesn't have the willpower to stay away from drugs," she added.

"Okay, wish me luck," Carrie said as she walked out the door.

"Good luck!" Sam and Emma called to her.

"Now, where were we?" Sam said, picking up the menu again.

Emma eyed Sam curiously. "Everything is very simple to you, isn't it? Very black and white."

"Sometimes," Sam agreed. "This time it is. No way should Carrie risk her career for Graham. Graham is responsible for himself."

Sam turned back to the menu, but Emma had lost her appetite. What if Carrie really had to choose between her friend and her career?

SEVEN

"Oh, Carrie, nice of you to join us," Faith
O'Connor said sarcastically as Carrie, Emma,
and Sam entered Graham's dressing room
backstage at the Miami Convention Center.

Carrie attempted a smile, then busied
herself with one of her cameras so she
wouldn't have to face Faith.

Everything was awful. Carrie had gone
back to the cocktail party, and had done as
Emma suggested, deliberately missing any
shot of Graham that could be incriminating.
It had become more and more difficult, since
Graham kept disappearing more often into
the bathroom as the party went on. Claudia
had tried to prevent him from doing that,
but he had given her defiant looks, seem-
ingly daring her to say anything. Everybody

had studiously avoided mentioning it. After all, Graham was the star.

Graham's dressing room (actually a suite) was a buzz of activity. Unlike many other stars, Graham shared his dressing room with his band. They sat around the room, some with instruments in hand, the drummer drumming with some pencils on a coffee table. Various girls and women hung around them. Two of them were wives traveling with their husbands; others were groupies, hangers-on who would do anything to be near the limelight. Faith sat near Graham, pen and pad in hand, speaking to him quietly. Mark hovered nearby. In thirty minutes Johnny Angel was scheduled to begin the concert. Carrie had deliberately waited as long as possible to show up backstage.

"Hi, love," Graham said, smiling at Carrie from the leather couch in the corner.

"Hi," Carrie said softly. Graham looked tired, the lines in his tanned face prominent. Carrie lifted her camera and clicked off some shots.

Claudia came in from the bathroom, a wet washcloth in her hands. She went to Graham and placed it on his forehead. "Better?" she asked him.

"Listen, Graham, we don't have to talk any more right now if you're too tired," Faith told Graham solicitously.

"No, it's cool," Graham said.

"Okay, then," Faith said with a smile. "I wanted to talk about your famous antidrug campaign."

A muscle twitched in Graham's cheek. "What about it?" he asked with an edge in his voice.

"You're very strongly against drugs, aren't you?" Faith asked innocently. Carrie tried to ignore her. Emma and Sam busied themselves pouring juice from the iced pitcher on the table. "I mean, at this point, after associating yourself so closely with an antidrug message, any involvement in something like that would practically kill your career, wouldn't it?" she pressed.

Graham picked up the washcloth and threw it across the room. Then he jumped up and made a beeline for the bathroom.

Carrie turned to Faith. She knew Faith was going to demand that she shoot Graham's picture as he came out of the bathroom, just in case there were any telltale signs of drug use. "Look, Faith, I'm sorry, but I just can't do this," Carrie began.

"Not to worry," Faith said, standing up and facing Carrie. "You're fired."

Sam and Emma stopped even pretending not to hear what was going on. They turned to face Faith and Carrie. Mark stood behind Faith, staring at the floor in embarrassment.

"I'm *what?*" Carrie asked incredulously.

Sam stepped up next to Carrie. "You can't do that!" she objected.

"Right, you can't do that," Emma agreed, moving to the other side of her friend. "She has a contract," Emma added, hoping that was true.

Carrie winced. She didn't in fact have a contract. There had been no time.

"Oh, don't worry, we won't screw you financially," Faith said. "You'll still get paid. I just don't intend to use your shots. This is too important. I've hired another photographer."

As Carrie stood there, too stunned to speak, the door to the suite banged open and two people ran in.

"Say cheese, babe!" a voice boomed, and a camera clicked off a shot of all of them standing with their mouths hanging open.

There behind the camera, in an Armani

suit and a silk shirt open to the waist, was Flash Hathaway. And if that wasn't bad enough, standing next to him, wearing the latest Givenchy flare minidress that sold for something in the four-digit range, was the one and only Lorell Courtland.

For a moment no one could speak. It was as if Carrie, Sam, and Emma's worst nightmare had just come true.

It was sleazy Flash who had taken the nearly nude shots of Sam, and then displayed them without her permission at a private club. And it was he who had expected Sam to sleep with him when he booked her for her first professional modeling shoot, and had fired her on the spot when she'd refused. Sam had gotten back at him, though. She'd arranged to have an item printed in the *Breakers*, Sunset Island's newspaper, that warned all the girls on the island about Flash's tactics. When the article appeared Flash had left Sunset Island abruptly, and Sam hadn't seen or heard from him since. Until now.

And then there was the inimitable Lorell Courtland. The girls had met Lorell at the au pair convention in New York the previous spring. Lorell was a perfectly groomed

Southern belle from Atlanta, and all she had seemed to talk about at the convention was how rich her family was, and how she didn't intend to actually have to *work* if she got hired as an au pair (she was only applying, she had told them, because her daddy thought it would "build her character"). Lorell's obnoxiousness being patently obvious, no one had hired her as their au pair. Her father, however, had fixed it so that Lorell could spend the summer living with the Popes, rich friends of his with a summer mansion on Sunset Island. Allegedly Lorell was supposed to be a role model for their shy, chubby, introverted twelve-year-old daughter, Alexa.

Lorell, it turned out, was friends with Emma's most-hated enemy from boarding school, Diana De Witt. Emma had been set on not letting anyone on the island know that she came from one of the wealthiest families in the country, because she was afraid they would treat her differently. Lorell had guessed who Emma really was, and Diana had confirmed it for her. Then Lorell had invited Diana to the island, just to embarrass Emma in front of everyone. It had worked. It had been humiliating for

Emma, and she'd almost lost her friends, as well as her boyfriend, Kurt, over all the misunderstandings. Even after that, Lorell Courtland, Diana, and their friend Daphne Whittinger had spent the rest of the summer doing everything they could to be hateful to Emma, Sam, and Carrie.

Flash and Lorell looked just as shocked at seeing Sam, Emma, and Carrie. Evidently this was a surprise to everyone.

"What are you, like some kind of plague thing, following me around, ruining my life?" Flash demanded, staring at Sam.

"You know her?" Faith asked.

"Unfortunately the answer is yes," Flash answered, "and may I add, a real pleasure it ain't."

Sam turned to Faith. "Tell me you didn't hire *him* to replace Carrie," she said.

"I don't need to tell you anything," Faith snapped, "but yes, Flash is the new photographer."

"Listen, Faith, I'm sure I got some great shots of Graham—" Carrie began.

"Which should be nice for your scrapbook," Faith finished for her.

"At least use both of them," Emma suggested.

Faith gave a small laugh. "I could," she agreed, "but I'm not going to."

Graham came out of the bathroom sniffing, with a big grin on his face. He headed back over to Faith at a gallop. Now he seemed suffused with a manic energy. The guys in his band assiduously looked away from him. "Sorry to interrupt the interview," Graham said smoothly. He didn't seem to notice that everyone was standing around looking uncomfortable, nor did he notice the two new people in the room. "Say, I've got a great idea! I've rented a yacht for after the show tonight. I thought it would be a nice idea to get out on the water with the guys. Why don't you all come and we can continue the interview there?"

"Oh, I imagine Faith and Carrie will be exhausted by that time, won't you?" Claudia said, coming up next to Graham and taking his arm.

"Not at all," Faith answered smoothly. "I'm sure we'd love to come. Right, Carrie?"

"But I thought I was—"

"Oh, I've asked another photographer to take a few shots, too," Faith said, interrupting Carrie. "You can never get too many great shots of a superstar," she explained.

105

"Flash Hathaway, this is Graham Perry and his wife, Claudia."

Flash stuck out his hand and pumped Graham's hand hard. "It's a true pleasure to meet a star of your caliber," Flash gushed. "Oh, and your old lady, too," he added.

"Great!" Graham said. "So everyone will come out on the boat, and we'll have a party!"

The door opened again and Johnny Angel entered, his eyes scanning the room until they lit on Sam.

"Hi there," he said in a low voice, coming up beside her. He was dressed for his show. His black sleeveless T-shirt was cut low, revealing a muscular, tanned chest that was already covered in sweat. His ripped, faded jeans clung to his legs like a second skin. "I was just warming up, and I thought I'd come see if you'd been only a figment of my imagination this afternoon."

"I'm real," Sam promised.

Johnny put one hand gently to Sam's neck and lifted her heavy red curls. "Yep, feels real, all right."

"Hey, have a good one out there tonight," Graham said to Johnny, offering his hand.

Johnny shook it. Carrie and Flash both

lifted their cameras and took shots at the same time. "Thanks, man. It's a real pleasure to be opening for you. I mean, I've admired your work since I was a little kid."

Graham smiled. "You make me sound like I should be carved on Mount Rushmore," he said.

Johnny laughed. "Hey, I didn't mean you were old—"

"Don't worry about it," Graham said, waving away Johnny's explanation. "Listen, we're all going out on this yacht I rented tonight after the gig. Why don't you and your band join us?"

Johnny's face lit up at the invitation. "Sounds cool," Johnny said. He looked at Sam. "You going?"

"I might," Sam answered.

Johnny gave her a heart-melting grin and leaned even closer. "Just remember, 'Breathless for You,'" he whispered, then ambled toward the door.

"I've still got a few minutes before I need to warm up," Graham told Faith. "Or are you sick of hearing about me?" he added charmingly.

"That wouldn't be possible," Faith said with a grin. She and Graham headed over to the couch in the corner. Claudia trailed after them, looking forlorn. Flash followed on Faith's heels, leaving Lorell standing there by herself.

Carrie stared at Mark. "Now what am I supposed to do?" she demanded.

"Keep taking pictures," Mark suggested. "Maybe they'll be so good that Faith'll be forced to use some of them."

Carrie sighed and walked over to Faith, steering as far away from Flash as possible.

Emma just stared at Lorell. Sam was rooted to the floor, gazing at the door through which Johnny Angel had just exited.

"What are you doing here?" Emma finally demanded of Lorell. "You're about the last person on earth I expected to see."

"Oh, believe me," Lorell began in her nasal, singsong drawl, "seein' the three of you is not my idea of a good time, either. Y'all are like some kind of awful recurrin' rash. It just keeps on comin' back."

"Johnny likes me," Sam said, ignoring Lorell and Emma completely. "He really, really likes me!"

"Please save the folksy sayings for someone who might find them something other than nauseating," Emma told Lorell.

Lorell pushed part of her perfect raven-colored bob behind one ruby-and-emerald-studded ear. "For your information," Lorell said with dignity, "I'm here with my boyfriend, Flash."

Emma nudged Sam to pull her attention away from the door and her thoughts about Johnny. "Sam, Lorell is here with her *boyfriend*, Flash," she repeated for Sam's benefit.

That got Sam. She turned to Lorell. "Your *boyfriend?* That's one of the funniest things I've ever heard in my life!"

"He happens to be a misunderstood genius," Lorell said with dignity.

Both Sam and Emma snorted back laughter. "Really?" Sam asked, wide-eyed. "And just how did you discover that?"

"Oh, I don't expect a person like you to understand," Lorell trilled to Sam. "After the shameless way you threw yourself at him back on Sunset Island—"

"I *what?*" Sam screeched.

"Everyone knew, so don't think you fooled anybody by gettin' that silly story printed in the *Breakers*. Trash talkin' trash, that's all it was."

Sam made a move for Lorell, but Emma stopped her. "Oh, come on, Sam, you can't possibly take Lorell seriously. Can't you see how funny this is?" Emma turned back to Lorell. "So, just how did you and Flash happen to find each other?"

"Just serendipity, I guess," Lorell gushed. "Flash came to Atlanta and took some modeling shots of my cousin, Muffy Sue."

"Yeah, and tell me he didn't put the moves on little old Muff—" Sam jeered.

"Muffy Sue is only six years old," Lorell said with dignity. "She won the Little Miss Sweetheart Contest sponsored by Universal Models. They sent Flash to take her portfolio shots. I saw him at her photo shoot, and one thing just led to another," Lorell explained. "I've been travelin' with him ever since."

"Oh, I bet Daddy is just thuh-*rilled* with that!" Sam said, and laughed.

Lorell looked at the floor briefly, then back at Sam. "No, he isn't," she confessed. "In fact, he's threatened to send some deprogrammers after me to kidnap me, since he says Flash must be one of those hypnotic gurus. I've tried to explain that this is nothing like that. This is love."

"Love?" Emma gulped.

"Love," Lorell confirmed, her eyes shining. "I've found the love of my life."

"Yo, babe, get me some toilet paper or somethin'. I got some kind of crap on this lens," Flash yelled to Lorell across the room.

"Of course, angel," Lorell purred, trotting to the bathroom.

"I wouldn't believe this if I weren't seeing it with my own eyes," Emma said, shaking her head.

"Me neither. But I'm too happy about Johnny to get all bent out of shape over Flash," Sam said. "Anyway, there's some kind of poetic justice about Lorell ending up with him."

"True," Emma agreed. "It's just that sometimes truth is really stranger than fiction."

"Here you go, lamby-pie," Lorell said, handing Flash the tissue.

"Make sure you stay out of the way," Flash told Lorell. "I'm tryin' to create here." Lorell started back toward Sam and Emma.

"And don't go near Big Red." he added referring to Sam. "She's off-limits."

Lorell stepped hastily away from Sam and Emma and headed over to the table to pour herself a drink.

"I'm going backstage to watch Johnny's set," Sam said. "Want to come?" she asked Emma.

"In a sec. I just want to check that Carrie's okay," Emma said.

"All right. See you there," Sam promised. She walked by Lorell, who was demurely sipping a glass of orange juice. "Fetch, Lorell! Fetch! Good doggie," she added wickedly, and sashayed out of the dressing room.

Over by the sofa, Graham stood up and stretched. "Let's stop until later," he suggested. "I'd like to spend a little time alone before I go on."

"Oh, of course," said the ever-solicitous Faith, standing up also. "We'll just go watch Johnny's set, then." She shot Flash a look that told him to follow Graham, who was heading for the bathroom.

Flash rushed over so fast that Graham practically ran into him. "Hey, man, I'm going to the head. Do you mind?"

"Big sorries, my man," Flash said, all smiles. "Just lookin' for the great shots, you know."

"Let's get some shots of the band," Faith said. She gave Carrie a pained look. "You might as well do that," she conceded. Carrie was so happy that Faith might use some of her shots after all that she immediately began to click away at the guys sprawled on various couches and chairs.

"Flash, why don't you go catch Johnny's set? Maybe we can get some great angles from backstage," Faith suggested.

"You got it," Flash agreed.

Flash, Lorell, and Emma headed through the maze of halls to the backstage area. Johnny Angel was just taking the stage, to the roar of thousands of fans. Somehow Sam had ended up on the other side of the stage, where Emma could barely see her. Emma sent her a little wave. Manic Sam waved back with excitement.

"Get that bimbo out of my viewfinder," Flash snarled, aiming his camera at Johnny as the singer broke into his first song.

Emma ignored him and listened to Johnny. His first tune was as uptempo and rocking as a tune could be, and it featured incredible gymnastic dancing on the part of Johnny and his three female backup dancers.

"He really moves well, doesn't he?" Emma remarked.

Flash laughed. "You got a great way of puttin' things, blondie."

"Emma," Emma corrected him.

"Sure, I remember your name," Flash said. "I remember a lot about you. Like how you always got that perpetual virgin look about you."

Emma looked at him. "You know, I thought I remembered how much of a total boor you are, but I was wrong. You're even worse than I recalled."

Flash bellowed a laugh and clicked off some more shots. "I gotta admit, I like the way you put things, even when it's an insult. Somehow from you it's sexy."

"Believe me, I don't consider that a compliment," Emma said icily.

Flash laughed again. "Hey, Lorell, get a load of her! She out-snobs you!"

"She just doesn't appreciate you as an artist, lamby-pie," Lorell trilled, shooting Emma the evil eye.

"Confidentially," Flash continued, ignoring Lorell, "I always wondered what a class act like you was doing' hangin' out with a lowlife like Big Red."

"Her name is Sam," Emma fumed, "and she happens to be one of my best friends."

"Whatever," Flash said with a shrug. "Whoa, that brunette dancer in the middle just about lost her hooters out of her tank top on that last jump—what a shot that would have been!"

On the other side of the stage, Sam was watching Johnny in a state of total bliss.

"Thanks a lot," Johnny was saying into the mike as the applause died down. "This next tune is one you might recognize." The band started to play the opening chords to "Breathless for You," the lighting changed to a sexy soft spot, and Johnny grabbed the microphone. Right before he starting singing, he looked offstage at Sam and winked. Then his husky, sexy voice filled the air.

"Jeez, the guy is a big star, and he's swooning for that bimbo redhead," Flash snorted. "Wait till I give the guy a clue, like maybe describing how she looks in a see-through leopard-print G-string."

Emma grabbed Flash's camera and twisted the strap around his neck.

"What the—" he choked out.

"My friend is not a bimbo and you will say *nothing*, you disgusting pig, or I will personally see that you are ruined. Believe me, I can do it," Emma said coolly. She stared into his rapidly reddening face. Usually she hated using any tactics that her mother might use, but at this particular moment there was a certain thrill in knowing that with the power and money of her family, she actually could make her threat come true.

Even Lorell knew it was so. She didn't say a word.

EIGHT

"Night of fire, heart's desire, only you can take me higher . . . I'm breathless, breathless for you!" Sam sang at the top of her lungs along with the radio as the three girls drove toward the marina after the concert.

"Tell me this isn't just like a movie!" Sam shouted over the blaring radio. "Johnny Angel just sang this song to me, and now I'm hearing it on the radio right before I go to a party with him on Graham Perry's yacht!"

"What street do I turn on again?" Carrie asked Emma, who was holding the directions the road manager had written out for them.

"It's a right on Cove, then a left on Marina Drive," Emma said, turning down the radio so Carrie could hear her.

Sam reached from the back seat and cranked the radio back up for the finish of the song. "I'm breathless, baby, breathless for you!" she sang.

Carrie winched. "No offense, Sam, but you dance a lot better than you sing."

"He just sings in the wrong key for me!" Sam said, sounding hurt.

Emma turned the radio back down to a reasonable level. "Sorry, Sam, but it's killing my ears up here. Oh, Carrie, there's the turn!" she added quickly, pointing to the street sign.

"Ha!" Sam said, sitting back and folding her arms. "You're just jealous, that's what it is," she said to Emma. "I mean, a gorgeous superstar is crazy about me, and you've got the Flashman panting after you!" Sam caught Carrie's eye in the rearview mirror and winked.

Emma winced. The last part of what Sam had said was true. No matter how much Emma insulted or threatened Flash, he kept flirting with her. After the concert he'd followed her around and made insinuating remarks, embarrassing her in front of everyone.

"Look, Flash is a disgusting toad, but I'm not jealous about you and Johnny," Emma said. "I'm happy for you."

"Me, too," Carrie said. "But I also think you should be careful, Sam," she added. "Don't let him break your heart."

"Hey, he'd better be careful that I don't break *his* heart!" Sam crowed.

A car honked from behind them, and then sped up to their right. Flash stuck his head out the window and waved at Emma. "Yo, blondie! Lookin' good, babe!"

Emma immediately pressed the button to raise her window and ignored him completely. This only made Flash crack up with laughter, swerve in front of their car, and careen off toward the marina.

"He may be the most loathsome person I have ever met," Emma remarked.

Sam leaned forward and whispered in Emma's ear, "He wants you, *babe*."

Emma swatted at Sam, who feinted away from her and laughed hysterically. "Come on, Em, you said yourself I shouldn't get upset over him, so neither should you," Sam said. "I can't even believe that it was only a few months ago that I fell for his stupid line about making me into a big model. I was such a kid then!"

"Do you think Faith will really use all his shots and none of mine?" Carrie asked nervously.

"Your shots will probably be so much better than Flash's that in the end she'll decide to use yours," Emma said loyally.

"I wish there was some way I could keep Flash from taking any shots that will really hurt Graham," Carrie mused. "Then no matter what Faith might want to imply in her exposé, she won't have any kind of photographic evidence."

"Fat chance you have of convincing Flash not to do something that could benefit his career, no matter how unethical it might be," Sam said.

"Sam's right," Emma said sadly. "He clearly only cares about himself."

"Oh, I don't know," Sam teased. "He might be willing to edit out those shots of Graham if you'll only spend one night of magic in his arms, blondie."

Emma looked horrified, and Carrie laughed as she turned the car onto Marina Drive, which ran parallel to the water.

"Wow, this is gorgeous," Carrie breathed

as they drove slowly down the road. On their right the water twinkled in the moonlight.

"This is it," Emma said, pointing to a large wooden sign that read HAULOVER MARINA. "We're supposed to look for slip fifty-seven."

"What's a slip?" Sam asked. "I mean, besides a quaint undergarment my mother still wears under dresses."

Emma laughed. "A slip is basically a parking spot for boats," she explained. "Normally it's shaped like the letter U, and the boat docks inside the U."

"Do you know a lot about boats?" Carrie asked Emma.

"Oh, just a little," Emma said.

"Don't tell me," Sam said. "You have your own yacht, called the *Emma*, where you've gone for jaunts with royalty, right?"

"It's my parents' yacht, and it's called the *Princess*," Emma admitted with a small smile. "I don't think Princess Di had been on it, but Fergie once got so sunburned on board that we had to dock and call a doctor."

Sam leaned forward and looked at Carrie. "Is she kidding?"

"I don't think so," Carrie answered.

"What's the number on that slip, Em?" she asked.

"Twenty-seven," Emma said. "It must be farther down."

Sam shook her head. "I can't imagine what it must be like to be you," she said to Emma. "So where is this yacht?"

"They keep it at Buzzard's Bay, south of Cape Cod," Emma said. "I used to spend summers there when I was a kid," she reminisced. "Sometimes I'd go out on the *Princess*, but more often I'd take the *Free Spirit* out—that's my dad's sailboat—and sail out until all I could see around me was ocean."

"By yourself?" Carrie asked.

"Sometimes, and sometimes with Dad," Emma said. "My mother never went because the wind would mess up her hair. My dad taught me to sail when I was twelve. It's really the only thing we ever did together. He was always working, and I was always away at school in Europe."

"There's number fifty-seven," Sam said, pointing out the window. She stuck her head out. "Omigod, is that *it*?"

The three girls stared out at a huge white yacht, lit up with tiny lights whose reflections twinkled in the water. Standing in front of the yacht were some of the guys from Graham's band, and Flash and Lorell were just climbing on board.

"That must be it," Carrie said, parking the car.

"Pinch me, I can't believe this is happening!" Sam cried.

Emma obliged and pinched Sam's arm as they got out of the car, but Sam was so awestruck that she never even felt it.

"I mean, Robin Leach could pop out of the bushes and interview us for *Lifestyles of the Rich and Famous!*" Sam rhapsodized. "This is definitely how I was meant to live."

Carrie got her cameras from the trunk, and the girls headed toward the yacht.

"Hi," Mark said when they got close to the boat. "I see you guys found it okay."

"We got good directions," Carrie assured him. "Where's Faith?"

"She's already on board," Mark said. "I was waiting for you."

"Why?" Carrie asked bluntly. Mark seemed like a nice guy, but he certainly didn't seem to be willing to help her stand up to Faith.

"Hey, look, she's my boss," Mark said in a low voice, obviously knowing exactly what was on Carrie's mind. "There's only so much I can do without risking my own butt."

"Fine," Carrie said tersely. "You certainly don't owe me anything." She started up the ramp toward the yacht.

"Carrie, wait!" he called to her, but Carrie just kept walking.

"Good for you," Emma said with approval.

"Thanks," Carrie said.

"Hey, Mark is a nice guy!" Sam objected.

"But Emma is right," Carrie insisted. "Sometimes you just have to take a stand. If Mark thinks that something Faith says to do is unethical, then he should stand up to her."

"And lose his job?" Sam asked incredulously. "Do you know many people would kill to work at *Rock On?*"

"Some things are more important than that," Emma responded self-righteously.

"Sometimes you just kill me, Emma," Sam said, shaking her head.

The girls were helped onto the yacht by a dashing-looking man with silver hair, dressed in an immaculate white uniform. "Good evening, ladies," he said smoothly. "I'm Captain Randall. Welcome aboard the *Vestal Virgin.*"

"Yo, blondie! I think the captain named

his ship after you!" Flash bellowed in Emma's face.

"Please," Emma said, stepping away from Flash. "Don't you find it embarrassing to have absolutely no class whatsoever?"

"Now, now," Sam chided Emma. "Flash has a lot of class. It's just that all of it is third!"

Everyone within hearing distance cracked up at that, except Lorell, who looked as if she would gladly scratch Sam's eyes out for insulting her man.

"Did you say something witty?" Flash asked, a feigned look of puzzlement on his face. "Like, do I know you or something? Oh, yeah!" he said, snapping his fingers. "You're that no-talent bimbo who wants to be a model. I didn't recognize you with your clothes on."

Before Sam could even form a retort, Lorell had hooked her arm through Flash's and was steering him away. "Bye-bye, girls!" she drawled happily, obviously thrilled that Flash had gotten in the last word.

"They are what I would call a match made in heaven," Carrie opined, watching them leave.

"I hope they both fall overboard," Sam muttered. "Maybe I could help."

"Forget them," Emma counseled. "Let's go find the party."

"You'll find the guests downstairs," Captain Randall said. "Just walk aft to the stern, and you'll see the companionway."

"What did he say?" Sam whispered to Emma.

"He said the stairs are at the back of the yacht," Emma translated.

"Well, why didn't he just say that?" Sam huffed as they made their way downstairs.

The party was already in full swing. A Garth Brooks CD blared through the sound system. Two tuxedoed bartenders stood behind a full bar, pouring drinks. A huge buffet table ran along one side of the room, covered with the finest crystal bowls and bone-china platters. The buffet offered everything from canapés to dessert. It began with the finest imported caviar overflowing from crystal goblets at one end of the table and finished at the other end with petit fours that had the *VV* crest of the *Vestal Virgin* traced in icing on top.

"Gee, Sam, they even made enough food

for you!" Carrie said, teasing Sam about her gargantuan appetite.

"Hmmm," Sam answered distractedly. She was eyeing Johnny Angel across the room. The singer was talking to a very attractive blonde.

"I think we've found something even more important to Sam than nourishment!" Emma said, laughing.

"I'm going back up to get some shots of the water," Carrie said.

"Faith won't care about that," Sam said.

"No, but I will," Carrie said, disappearing up the stairs.

"Do you think she's good-looking?" Sam asked Emma, anxiously eyeing the blonde with Johnny. He whispered something in the blonde's ear, and she threw her head back and laughed.

"Not even in your league," Emma assured Sam.

"You're sure?" Sam asked, licking her lips nervously. Suddenly she didn't feel so very confident after all.

"I'm sure," Emma said.

"The important thing is, he can't know how much I want him," Sam murmured fervently. She looked around just as two members of Graham's band were walking by.

"Oh, hi, Kyle!" Sam said, giving Graham's bass player a radiant smile.

Kyle was an unbelievably excellent musician and had played with Graham for years, but around girls he was still painfully shy. Sam and Emma had gotten to know the guys in Graham's band while Carrie was his au pair. With Kyle was a younger, dark-haired guy who looked quite a bit like Kyle, only taller and cuter.

"Hi!" said Kyle, obviously thrilled with Sam's attention. "This is my brother, Chad," Kyle said. "He goes to the University of Miami, so I invited him to the gig tonight."

Sam and Emma introduced themselves.

"You know, you were fabulous tonight, just awesome!" Sam gushed, grinning down at Kyle, who was a couple of inches shorter than she. Emma couldn't help but notice that even as Sam talked to Kyle she kept one eye glued to Johnny across the room.

"Oh, well, it was a pretty good gig," Kyle said, smoothing back his thinning hair.

"I thought it was great, too," Chad agreed. "Would you like to dance?" he asked Emma. A few couples were now moving around the small dance floor to a slow tune.

"Sure," Emma said with a smile. *Chad was very cute*, she thought.

"So what's your connection to all this?" Chad asked as his arms went around Emma.

"I'm a friend of the photographer, who is a friend of Graham's," Emma explained.

"You're a friend of *his?*" Chad asked incredulously, looking down at Emma. At that moment Flash laughed loudly, and they both looked across the room, where he was eating a heaping mound of caviar off a small plate and talking with Faith O'Connor.

"Wrong photographer." Emma laughed. "My friend's name is Carrie Alden. She's on deck taking some shots."

Chad laughed, too. "I have to admit, I wondered there for a second. That guy introduced himself to me and two seconds later he was asking me where he could score some blow around here."

Emma stopped dancing. "He *what?*"

"He asked me where he could get some blow—you know, cocaine," Chad repeated. "Number one, I'm totally not into drugs, and number two, I don't even know the dude. Very weird!"

"Hi!" Sam called as she danced by with Kyle. She had a smile plastered to her face, but Emma could see how unhappy she was. Johnny Angel was still talking with the blonde. He hadn't made one move toward Sam.

"Yo, blondie!" Flash called to Emma as he danced Lorell closer to Emma and Chad. He dropped his arms from around Lorell and aimed his camera. "Give the Flashman that mine-doesn't-stink look!"

Emma stared at him, unbelievingly, as he snapped her picture.

"Stop that!" she said. He clicked another shot.

"Listen, you worm—" she began.

"Ooh, you turn me on when you're angry, babe," Flash said, taking two more shots.

"Hey, what's your problem, man?" Chad said, facing Flash. "She doesn't want you to take her picture, got it?"

Just at that moment Graham ambled into the room, heading for the bar. "Gotta run, duty calls," Flash said, dashing away. Lorell was left standing by herself on the dance floor.

"You should be honored to have a photographer of his stature take photos of you," Lorell managed. She shook her bobbed hair, sucked in her cheeks, and flounced away.

"Is she for real?" Chad asked Emma.

"Who knows?" Emma said.

They danced over toward where Kyle and Sam were talking. As they passed by they could hear Kyle saying earnestly to Sam, " . . . so then when I graduated from the Berklee School of Music I got into jazz." Sam kept nodding her head at him as though she was listening, but her eyes were darting around the room looking for Johnny.

"My older brother's the genius of the family," Chad said to Emma with a grin.

"He's a terrific musician," Emma agreed. "What are you studying?"

"Fine arts—I'm a painter," Chad said rue-fully, "which according to my father means I'm studying to be unemployed. How about you?"

"French," Emma admitted.

"Hey, cool," Chad said.

"Not really," Emma admitted. "The truth of the matter is, it's boring me to death."

"Then why are you majoring in it?" Chad asked reasonably.

"It was my mother's idea," Emma admitted, rolling her eyes. "She was a French major, and *her* mother was a French major. It's just what the women in my family do."

"So you're studying something that bores you to death because your mother wants you to?" Chad asked incredulously.

"I suppose so," Emma agreed.

"I would never do that," Chad said fervently. "I'd rather starve than not pursue what's really important to me."

"Well, that's you," Emma said. "That's not me."

The song ended and segued into a rocking, up tempo number.

Chad stared at Emma. "So what *is* you, then?"

"Good question," Emma said lightly. "Let's take a walk," she suggested, eager to change the subject. She didn't really have any desire to bare her soul to Chad—not that she was sure exactly what was in her soul, anyway. Why did it seem much simpler for other people to figure their lives out?

They headed up the stairs and strolled slowly along the deck, enjoying the fresh, salty air.

"I was serious, you know," Chad said,

returning to their conversation. "What *is* you?"

"Oh, who knows?" Emma said. She stopped walking and leaned over the railing, staring out at the endless sea. It brought back memories of being with her father out on the water. Those were the only happy memories Emma had of her childhood. She'd listened so avidly to everything her father had taught her, wanting so much for him to approve of her, to love her. And so they had shared the sea, for a time, until the summer ended and Emma was banished once again to the Swiss boarding school she hated.

But how could she tell a guy she had just met any of that without sounding like some stupid, spoiled rich kid? *Which is probably exactly what I am*, Emma thought to herself, and sighed out loud.

"Hey, it's much too beautiful a night for pensive sighs," Chad remarked.

"You're right," Emma agreed softly, turning to look at him.

Chad leaned close and kissed Emma lightly on the lips.

"That was nice," Emma murmured.

"I agree," Chad said, and leaned over to kiss her again.

When they drew apart Emma shivered in the cool evening air.

"Cold?" Chad asked.

"A little," Emma said. She rubbed her arms briskly.

"I've got a jacket downstairs," Chad said. "I'll run down and get it for you. Be right back," he promised, and sprinted away.

Emma stared back out at the sea. She suddenly thought about Kurt Ackerman, the first—and so far the only—guy she had ever loved. Kurt loved the sea so much. He'd grown up in the small year-round community on Sunset Island, and the water had always been a big part of his life. But it was all over with Kurt, she had to remind herself. No matter how much she might still be in love with him, she had to stop thinking about him and move on with her life. Chad seemed like a nice guy, and she was having a good time, and she absolutely refused to let thoughts of Kurt ruin it.

The truth of the matter was, she didn't want to think at all. Not about Kurt, and not about college or her future, about which she didn't have a clue. She thought about her application to the Peace Corps, which still lay in the top drawer of her dresser.

When she'd returned to Boston at the end of the summer, she'd come so close to applying. Working on Sunset Island had made her feel better about herself. It had made her realize that she was more than just some spoiled rich girl, that she really could live up to such a challenge. But when she'd gone back to her old life, where she was surrounded by privilege and luxury, she'd quickly lost that self-confidence. And so she hadn't done anything at all, except hate herself for being who she was.

"You look lost in space," Chad remarked as he came up to her and put his jacket around her shoulders.

"Thanks," Emma said, smiling at him.

"Where were we?" he asked softly, and gently put his arms around her.

Kissing Chad was nice. Emma blocked out thoughts of anything else. *I'm just going to have fun*, she promised herself.

"You think you can get shots up here?" Graham asked Carrie as they walked on deck.

"I don't think there's enough light," Carrie said regretfully. "Too bad, because I think we could get some great stuff."

"Carrie, what are you doing with Graham?" Faith asked, hustling over to them.

"Setting up some shots," Carrie said innocently.

"I brought along enough lights to shoot Graham up here," Flash announced, coming up behind Faith. "No prob."

"Yeah, well, if it's all the same to you, I'd like Carrie to take the shots," Graham said. "No offense, man."

"I asked Flash to get the shots," Faith said. "I hope you understand. He's got a lot more experience than Carrie, and this is a major piece we're doing. Flash, get your lights."

"Can do," Flash assured Faith. He turned to Lorell, who was standing behind him. "Bring the extra lights up, babe. It's magic time!"

Graham looked at Flash. "Just out of curiosity, does everyone think you're a wanker, or is it just me?"

For a second, an almost frightened look crossed Flash's face.

"I, uh . . ." he stammered.

Graham turned to Faith. "If you want more shots of me, Carrie is taking them," he told her tersely. "I'll be back." He turned and walked quickly away.

"I guess we know where he's headed," Faith murmured to Flash, sniffing meaningfully.

"He was kidding, right?" Flash asked Faith.

"He's all coked up," Faith explained. "You have to take anything he says with a grain of salt." She moved closer to Flash. "I'm telling you, you get the shot I want, and I'll pay you double for this gig."

"I live but to serve, babe," Flash assured her.

"Just one thing," Faith added.

"Sure," Flash said easily.

"Don't ever, *ever* call me babe again. "Now go after Graham and see if you can get that shot."

"I'll get it," Flash promised, heading in the direction Graham had gone.

Faith watched Flash's retreating form. "He really *is* a wanker, isn't he?"

Carrie gathered up her courage and took a step toward Faith. "Listen, I really don't think you should do this to Graham," she said bravely.

Faith just looked at her. "You just don't

get it, do you?" she said. "*I'm* not doing anything to Graham. I didn't force him to take drugs, and no one else did, either. The bottom line is, Graham is doing it to himself."

Carrie had no comeback—because she knew that Faith was right.

NINE

". . . so then I started writing songs," Kyle was saying as he and Sam leaned on the bar. Sam's eyes were glazing over. Kyle might be a terrific musician, but he was also the most self-centered, boring person that she had ever met.

Sam finished her second glass of champagne and sighed. This was not going at all well. Johnny had danced three dances with the cute blonde, then they had gone for a walk up on the deck. Meanwhile, she was still downstairs in the main salon listening to Kyle talk about his musical career.

Somebody put Johnny Angel's CD on the stereo, and the sounds of "Breathless for You" filled the air.

"Dance?" Kyle asked.

Sam nodded her assent. Dancing was better than listening to the rest of Kyle's biography. Evidently Johnny hadn't been impressed that she was talking to an older guy who was a famous musician. The truth of the situation seemed to be that Johnny hadn't even noticed. *Well, as soon as this dance is over,* Sam vowed, *I'm going to excuse myself and at least find some more interesting company. After all, this is one wild party, and I'm not going to waste it mooning after Johnny Angel, that rotten, lying little—*

"Do you mind?" Johnny Angel said, tapping Kyle on the shoulder.

Kyle looked momentarily confused.

"I think this used to be called cutting in," Johnny said with an apologetic smile. "Anyway, this is Sam's song, and I promised I'd dance with her."

"Oh, okay," Kyle said easily. He drifted over to the bar.

Sam stood there, her hands on her hips. "I don't remember your promising to dance with me," she said. "And at any rate, I never promised to dance with you."

"Should I leave?" Johnny asked with a look of total innocence.

"Not necessarily," Sam said. "Maybe you should ask that blonde you've been talking to all night to dance."

Johnny put his arms around Sam—at which point she thought she'd die from happiness—and slowly started moving to the music. "Let's not waste the song, okay?" he said softly. Then he started singing in her ear, "Breathless, baby, breathless for you!"

Okay, Sam thought to herself, *a superstar is crooning his song into my ear. This is the highlight of my life to date.*

"You know, you sound a lot like Johnny Angel when you sing," Sam quipped. "Has anyone ever told you that?"

Johnny smiled but didn't answer. He just quietly sang the rest of the song in Sam's ear.

The next song was "Restless," the most jumping cut on the album. Sam spun away from Johnny and started to dance, letting the music flow through her. She was so happy—not to mention fueled by two glasses of champagne—that she threw herself uninhibitedly into her dancing. Johnny watched her for a second, then joined her, improvising on the choreography he did to that number during his stage show. Sam picked up the basic step quickly and fell in beside him, adding her own twists and flourishes. People started gathering around, cheering them on, until a crowd of people were hooting and hollering their approval as Johnny and Sam danced. Johnny did a triple spin on the final chord, then whirled Sam around in his arms and dipped her back so that her hair brushed the ground on the last beat of the song.

Everyone started whistling and clapping, catcalling and yelling their approval. Johnny righted Sam and stood there, grinning at her.

"Girl, you are one terrific dancer!" he said.

Sam beamed at him. "You're not so bad yourself," she said.

"Let's go for a walk," he suggested. "I could use some air."

The crowd disappeared as Sam and Johnny headed for the deck. The air was cooler now. Sam lifted her hair and let the breeze blow on the back of her neck.

"I'm serious, you really are a great dancer," Johnny said, assessing Sam with curiosity.

"And here you thought I was just another pretty face," she jibed, leaning against the rail.

"I guess that's true," Johnny chuckled. "Did you ever think about doing it professionally?"

"I don't think about it, I do it," Sam said coolly.

"No kidding?" Johnny asked, looking surprised.

"What is it with you?" Sam asked, letting her hair fall down around her shoulders. "Do you just assume that you're the only person who does anything interesting with his life?"

Johnny had the grace to look chagrined. "It's just that a lot of the girls that hang around—well, no offense, but they don't necessarily have a lot of talent or brains."

"First of all," Sam said, "I was not 'hanging around.' You came to talk to me, if you recall. Second of all, you're a jerk, so goodbye." Sam turned on her heel and started away from Johnny.

He came up behind her quickly and caught her shoulder. "Hey, I'm sorry. Really. I apologize," he said. "I shouldn't have assumed—"

"Anything," Sam finished for him.

"Right, anything." Johnny grinned. Sam grinned back at him. "So, where do you dance?" he asked her.

"Disney World," she admitted. "But that's only a start. Someday I'll be on Broadway."

Johnny nodded seriously. "Hey, go for it! Most people don't have any idea what hard work it is, what kind of discipline it takes. I've been dancing since I was a kid, and believe me, a guy taking dancing lessons when the other guys are out playing football doesn't exactly get respect around the playground."

"I guess it's harder for a guy," Sam sympathized.

"I got my nose broken twice in grade school before I decked some kid for harassing me, and then that was that," Johnny told her.

"So how did you get into dancing?" Sam asked.

"My parents were professional ballroom dancers," Johnny said. "They competed all over the country, and had their own dance school back in my hometown." Johnny looked out at the sea, his eyes alight with

144

memories. "Man, I used to love to watch them dance. I thought my dad was better than Fred Astaire. And my dad was the most macho guy I knew, so I figured if it was cool for him to dance, it was cool for me."

"They must be really proud of you," Sam said softly.

"They died in a car accident last year," Johnny said quietly, "just before I got my record deal."

"Oh, I'm so sorry," Sam said, putting her hand on Johnny's arm.

"I like to think that they know, somehow," Johnny said.

"Maybe they do," Sam said gently.

Johnny put his arm around her shoulders and smiled sadly at her. "You're a very special girl, Sam."

She studied Johnny's profile as he stared out at the water. God, he was gorgeous. And so talented and sensitive. Any girl in America would be thrilled to change places with her. Here she was, Samantha Bridges of Junction, Kansas, out with the newest, finest rock star in America, and he was falling for her. *Her!*

"I never wanted to be ordinary," Sam

said. She was thrilled that Johnny saw how special she really was. "I'm going to see the whole world. I'm going to have great, exciting adventures."

Johnny looked at her, his eyes sparkling in the moonlight. "Is this an exciting adventure?" he asked her in a soft voice.

"It might be," Sam whispered.

She closed her eyes and Johnny softly kissed her lips. It was just as fabulous as she had imagined it would be. He didn't rush, or immediately force his tongue down her throat, or do any of the disgusting things other guys had done. Slowly, he tasted her lips, running his fingers gently through her hair. His mouth opened finally, and Sam's did, too, as Johnny pressed his body against hers. It might have been minutes, it might have been hours that they stood there, their arms wrapped around each other, kissing under the twinkling stars.

Johnny groaned softly under his breath, and Sam felt as if she couldn't catch her breath. Even her knees felt weak and trembly. Everything felt dangerous and wonderful and perfect.

"Do you know what you're doing to me?" Johnny asked in a husky voice.

"What?" Sam whispered.

Johnny groaned, and Sam smiled. This was glorious, this feeling of power. She was making the famous Johnny Angel groan with passion, and she was more turned on than she'd ever been in her life.

"Sam, I really want to—" Johnny began, but he was interrupted by Flash, who was dashing along the deck.

"Hey, Big Red, have you seen Graham?" Flash asked, ignoring the obvious—that he was breaking in on a very intimate scene.

"He went for a swim," Sam said dryly. "I suggest you follow him."

"Ooh, big laughs," Flash commented sarcastically. "Your sense of humor is almost as tiny as your hooters."

Flash dashed off before Sam could muster up a comeback. She was horribly embarrassed. She had noticed that the blonde Johnny had been with earlier had an impressive bustline, half of which had been on display in her brief halter top.

"Hostile dude," Johnny commented.

"He's a cretin," Sam said, trying to sound as if Flash's insult meant nothing to her. "He did some shots for my modeling portfolio a while back, and he's ticked off because I wouldn't let him get in my pants."

"So you model, too," Johnny said.

"Here and there," Sam said casually.

Johnny looked her over and nodded. "You're great-looking. You could probably make a fortune at it."

"Really?" Sam asked, thrilled at Johnny's compliment. Instantly she was angry at herself. That was not the cool way to act and cool seemed to be working like magic. "I mean," Sam corrected herself, "I hear that sort of thing all the time, you know?"

"Sure," Johnny agreed. "I want to be known for my talent, not how I happen to look."

"Right," Sam said, "that's how I feel, too."

Johnny moved closer again and kissed Sam's neck. He put his arms around her waist and let them travel down a few inches as he buried his face in her hair.

"Mmmmm, you smell great," he murmured.

He started kissing her again, softly. A thrill ran through Sam's body. It felt so good to be in Johnny's arms.

"I'm so glad I met you," Johnny whispered between kisses.

"Me, too," Sam said, kissing him back.

"You know, it really takes an artist to understand an artist," he said, nuzzling her neck. "We live life differently. It's hard for other people to understand our priorities, don't you think?"

"I know just what you mean," Sam whispered fervently.

"We don't follow the rules," Johnny said, running his hands down Sam's back. "We make our own, right?"

"We make our own," Sam echoed, giving herself up to Johnny's kiss. Her heart thudded in her chest. Every nerve in her body was alive, straining to be closer to him. They *did* make their own rules! They *were* different! Johnny understood her as no guy ever had before. He was a real artist, just like she was. This moment was clearly meant to be.

"I want to be alone with you," Johnny whispered in her ear.

"Me, too," Sam agreed.

Johnny's eyes searched her face, then without a word he took her by the hand.

He seemed to know his way around the yacht. He led her down a flight of stairs Sam

149

hadn't seen before, down a small hallway, and through a door. They were in a bedroom. A queen-size bed covered with a satin quilt filled the room.

Well, we certainly are alone, Sam thought. She hadn't realized when she'd agreed with Johnny just what "alone" might mean. She hadn't known a bedroom with an actual bed would be involved. She stood near the door and tried to look hip.

"Sam?" Johnny asked. He held out his hand and led her over to the bed, then sat down beside her. Johnny took her in his arms and held her against him, stroking her hair. *If only this moment could last, just exactly like this,* Sam thought.

"How did you know this room was here?" Sam whispered. Suddenly she wanted to talk.

"Graham took me on a tour of the boat before," Johnny said. "He's thinking of buying it."

"Oh. Do you think he should?" Sam asked. She knew it was a stupid question, but suddenly she didn't feel so fabulous. Not that she didn't want to be alone with Johnny, because she did, but she also felt like maybe she was getting in over her head.

"Does it matter?" Johnny asked.

Sam attempted a smile.

"You're nervous," Johnny said, accurately reading Sam's mood.

"Oh, well, you know . . ." Sam said lamely.

"Everything is okay," Johnny said quietly with his arms around her. "We won't do anything that you don't want to do."

One part of Sam felt better, and another part of her reminded her that she had heard that line from guys before, right before they tried to dive under her skirt.

But Johnny's different, she reminded herself. *He doesn't have to put any moves on me because he can get any girl he wants. He's much too cool to grope me.*

As if to illustrate Sam's thoughts, Johnny just held Sam, not moving except to stroke her hair, until she felt more comfortable, bold even. She started kissing him then. And he kissed her back.

The next thing she knew they were lying on the bed. At first she felt nervous again, but Johnny didn't go any further. Only the top halves of their bodies were touching. The kisses were exquisite, and eventually

Sam was more turned on than she was scared.

His hand roamed down to her breasts, caressing them softly.

"They're kind of small," Sam said nervously.

"Shhhh," Johnny crooned. "You're perfect, Sam, don't you know that?"

Fortunately Sam said *I am?* in her head instead of out loud. She didn't actually say anything out loud; she just breathed a lot. So did Johnny. This gave Sam some time to think.

I really, really, really want this guy, is what she thought. *He truly appreciates me. He's special, and he told me I'm special. Maybe we were meant to be together, two passionate artists, who make our own rules.*

Sam could feel Johnny's hand slowly moving from her waist to her belly. That had always been the red-light signal for her, the no-touching zone. But, she thought, passionate artists don't zone off their bodies like little children—you can touch this but not that—did they? This was the new Sam, the artist loved by an artist, who didn't have to follow any rules.

Gently Johnny sat Sam up, dropped her

suspenders, and took off her orange bra top. She wasn't wearing anything underneath. He pulled off his T-shirt and wrapped his arms around her.

"You're very beautiful," he whispered softly.

Sam heaved a sigh of relief. This was obviously the guy she had been waiting for forever. *Take that, you dweeby little guys back in Junction!* the voice in Sam's head shouted. *I'm about to lose my virginity to a major rock star who thinks I am a beautiful, special artist!*

Wait, did I just tell myself I'm about to lose my virginity? Sam asked herself. *Am I really going to, right here? Right now? Is this actually it?*

Sam and Johnny continued kissing, and the voice in Sam's head continued in earnest.

Hey, if this is actually it, the voice said, *you have to talk about birth control.*

Shut up, voice! Sam wanted to yell. *Can't I even get swept away like they do in the movies?*

No chance, the voice said. *Sex can be dangerous these days, especially with a superstar like Johnny Angel, who might have been with a lot of different girls.*

That's going to end, of course, Sam wanted to tell the voice. *After this we'll be a couple.*

Cool, babe, the voice said, *but let's deal with the moment.*

"Deal with the moment? What do you mean?" Johnny asked softly.

Suddenly she realized she'd spoken out loud. "I meant this is a special moment," Sam said quickly.

"Mmmmm, very special," Johnny murmured.

He kissed her in that way he had that made her feel as if she were careening down a roller coaster. It was scary and shivery and wonderful, all at the same time.

Still, she had to find a way to say what she had to say. *God, this is so embarrassing,* she thought. How did people actually talk about condoms? To begin with, it was such a stupid word. *Condom.* It sounded too much like *condemn,* which reminded her of what her mother would think of the situation she was in at that very moment, which wasn't any too romantic, thank you very much. Okay, she could opt for *rubber.* No, that was worse. She had a horribly uncool cousin in

England who always put rubbers on over her shoes when it rained. Maybe *protection* was good. She could ask him if he had protection. *Oh, very hip*, she told herself. *He might pull out some deodorant.*

Look, cut the running monologue and talk to the guy, that pesky inner voice insisted. *If you're old enough to do it, you're old enough to be responsible.*

Okay. Fine. I'll say it like it's no big deal, Sam decided, *like I've said it lots of times before. God forbid he should find out I'm a virgin.*

"Johnny, I, uh . . ." Sam stammered as Johnny's mouth did incredible things to the back of her neck.

There was a loud knock on the door.

Instinctively Sam sat up and covered herself with a pillow.

"Hey, I'm busy in here," Johnny called out. He put his arm around her protectively.

"I can see that," a female voice said dryly as the door was pushed open. There stood the blonde that Johnny had been talking with earlier.

"Hey, Linda, come on," Johnny exclaimed. The blonde ignored Johnny's objections and waltzed into the room. She stood over the bed and looked down at Sam. "Hello," she said with a British accent. "I'm Linda, Johnny's girlfriend."

TEN

For once in Sam's life she was too stupe-
fied to speak. She just sat there clutching
the pillow to her.

"Having a bit of fun?" Linda asked wickedly.

"Linda, this is so bogus of you—" Johnny
began.

"Nice master cabin," Linda said, looking
around the room. "Really plush."

"Would you please leave?" Johnny asked
her in a low voice.

"Leave?" Linda said, sounding surprised.
"Why would I do that? I mean, you *did* bring
me to this gig, love," she reminded Johnny.

Sam tried to keep herself covered with
one hand while she reached for her top with
the other.

"Looking for this, lovey?" Linda asked,

picking up Sam's orange bra top and dangling it on one finger, out of Sam's reach.

Sam wanted to cry. This couldn't possibly be happening to her. This girl was Johnny's *girlfriend*. He had brought her to the party. And Sam had been just about to . . . God, it was all too horrible.

"Having it off with a rock star, eh?" Linda asked Sam. "You groupies just can't seem to keep your hands off Johnny!"

"Look, just give me my top and let me get out of here," Sam said in a low voice.

"Funny, you weren't too anxious to leave a few moments ago," Linda said.

Johnny grabbed Sam's top and handed it to her, then he rather forcefully moved Linda toward the door. "I'll talk to you later," he told her.

"Oh, we'll do more than talk," she promised him. "Well, ta-ta, love!" she called to Sam. "We'll have to compare notes on him sometime."

Johnny shut the door and turned to Sam, who was scrambling into her top with trembling fingers.

"Sam, I—"

"Don't say anything," Sam insisted in a tight voice as she tried to straighten her clothes. All she could think about was getting out of the cabin as quickly as possible.

"I think that was Linda's idea of a joke," Johnny explained, walking over to Sam.

"Your girlfriend has a terrific sense of humor," Sam said, trying not to let her voice tremble. She finally got her top on and looked around for her purse.

"Please don't leave," Johnny said.

"Don't leave?" Sam echoed. "Are you nuts? Your girlfriend just caught us together half-naked, and you want me to hang out? Where the hell is my purse?"

Johnny found it under the edge of the bedspread and handed it to Sam. "I did bring her," Johnny admitted, "but she's not my girlfriend. I mean, we had a casual thing going a few months ago, but now we're friends. She happened to be in town. She called me at the hotel and asked to come along because she wanted to meet Graham."

"What were you doing in here with me when you brought another girl?" Sam demanded.

"I was enjoying you," Johnny said, "and I thought you were enjoying me. You were looking for excitement, you said."

"Is that what I was?" Sam asked. "Excitement?"

"The best kind of excitement," Johnny insisted. He reached for her hand. "Come on, Sam. You understand. I know you do. You're an artist, just like me. We play by our own rules, remember? I've got to put all my energy into building my career right now. Tomorrow I'll be in a different town, and who knows where the day after that. But that doesn't mean I don't have any feelings for you."

"Right," Sam scoffed with a laugh. Unfortunately the sound came out more like a cry.

"It doesn't mean that you aren't special, Sam," Johnny said gently, "because you are." Sam was trying desperately not to cry as Johnny peered into her eyes. "Hey, I thought you understood," he said. "You acted like you did."

"Cool," Sam managed to say, pulling her hand away from Johnny's. "I've got to go." Sam headed for the door.

"Hey, Sam, I'm really sorry if I hurt you. I—"

But Sam couldn't hear the rest of what Johnny said. She was running out of the cabin, down the narrow hall, as fast as she could.

"Oh, I see we're all buttoned up again, aren't we?" Linda's voice chirped as Sam flew by her in the hall.

Sam ignored her and rushed by, willing herself not to cry until she could find some place private. She found a door that she remembered led to a bathroom, and she pulled it open. On the other side of the door was Lorell. *She looks like hell*, it occurred to Sam briefly, with some small area of her brain that wasn't occupied with her own misery.

Lorell was startled to see Sam there, too, but she quickly regained her composure. Lorell was indeed miserable—for the past ten minutes she had been holed up in the bathroom crying her eyes out. She really loved Flash, and there he was spending the evening ignoring her and chasing after Emma Cresswell. It was just so humiliating. If there was one thing Lorell Courtland had never had to put up with, it was humiliation.

"Hey, Sammi," Lorell purred, quickly setting her jaw so that Sam wouldn't see how upset she was. Lorell eyed Sam critically.

She took in the anguish on Sam's face, the mascara under her eyes, her disheveled clothing.

"You look like doggie doo," she pronounced happily, "if you don't mind my tellin' you so as a friend."

"That's pretty funny coming from a girl low enough to pant after Flash Hathaway," Sam managed, biting her lower lip to keep it from trembling.

Lorell went quickly for the jugular, as if she was afraid Sam might actually be right. "You're just tryin' to cover up how you threw yourself at Flash back on the island," Lorell said, adding, "just like you've been throwin' yourself at that rock star Johnny Angel all night."

"That's not true," Sam said.

"Of course it's true," Lorell jeered. "Everyone on the yacht is laughin' at you. A guy like Johnny Angel would only be interested in trash like you for one thing, and from the looks of you he already got that."

Sam ran, blindly careening into people and walls. She could hear Lorell's jeering voice echoing in her ears. Everyone was laughing at her. She had made a total fool out of herself, acting as if a rock superstar like Johnny Angel would actually become her boyfriend.

"I'm so stupid," Sam cried, tears blurring everything around her. She ran up to the deck, but the sounds of music and laughter grew closer. Where could she run to? Where could she escape?

"Oh, jeez, it's Big Red," she heard Flash's voice taunt from behind her. "Hey, ain't it funny, them letting her on a boat called the *Vestal Virgin?*"

Sam thought she heard some people laughing, but she didn't stop to see. She just ran to the back of the yacht, away from everyone.

"Sam, hi! Where have you been?" Carrie asked. She was standing alone, taking a picture of the moonlit water.

Sam rushed past Carrie, barely seeing her. She just had to be alone, somewhere, somehow. Dimly she heard Carrie calling to her, but she didn't stop running. How could she ever face her friends again? Carrie and Emma had tried to warn her, but no, she had told them she knew just what she was doing. Everyone must think she was the biggest idiot in the world, and she thought so, too.

When she reached the rear deck of the yacht, all she wanted was to jump into the water, just to get away from everyone and everything. Sam grasped the rail and looked down, sobs racking her. Then she noticed a metal ladder leading down to a small boat that rocked gently in the water.

Without thinking, Sam climbed over the rail onto the ladder. She clambered down until she could easily step into the small boat. Finally, she was alone. She huddled up in a corner and let the tears take over. She felt as if she could never face anyone again.

Back on the yacht, Emma was taking a stroll with Chad. They had kissed in a dark corner over and over, and it had been wonderful, but Emma was not interested in going any further. She thought a walk might cool them both off. They ran into Carrie on the port side.

"Hi, get any good shots of Graham?" Emma asked.

"I think I did, actually," Carrie said. "Not that I think Faith will use them."

"Yeah, Flash has been dogging him all

164

night," Emma said with a sigh. "The only good thing about it is it means he occasionally leaves me alone."

"There's no way I can stop him from getting incriminating shots of Graham," Carrie sighed. "I can't stand the idea that Graham's career could be ruined just because Faith wants a scoop." She stared out at the water. "It's just so . . . so mean. Graham's a great guy. How can Flash take advantage of him if he's having a problem with drugs?"

Chad laughed. "I'm sorry, but it's funny coming from Flash. Like I told Emma, he asked me for some coke before. I think he thought I was a roadie or something."

"Flash asked you for drugs?" Carrie asked. "You mean he's willing to ruin someone else's career when he's got the same problem himself?"

"Evidently," Emma said dryly. "Such a charming fellow."

"You're sure about this?" Carrie asked.

"I'm sure he asked," Chad said. "I couldn't swear as to why."

Carrie looked thoughtful. "What if . . . what if we bluffed him? What if we said that unless he turned over the shots of Graham to us, we'd blow the whistle on him?"

"You think that would work?" Chad asked.

"It might work if I did it," Emma said. "He's scared of me."

Chad smiled and ran his hand along the back of Emma's neck. "Oh, really I can see how he might want to be stuck on a desert island with you, but I don't see him being scared of you."

"He is," Emma insisted. "He knows I can ruin him. I'm telling you, I think it will work."

"Emma, no offense, but—" Chad began.

"She can do it," Carrie interrupted Chad. "Take her word for it."

"Hey, come on," Chad said. "Who's got that kind of power, besides the president or the Mafia? Is your dad in the Mafia?" Chad joked.

"The Mafia is scared of my father," Emma said evenly.

Chad made a disbelieving face. "Yeah, sure. I guess your last name is Kennedy or Rockefeller," he joked.

"No, but they're friends of my family," Emma said lightly.

"She's kidding, right?" Chad asked Carrie,

but Carrie didn't answer him. She was busy staring at Emma.

"Are you sure you want to do something like that?" Carrie asked. "I mean, I know how much you hate having people see you as different because of your money—"

"Jeez, she's telling the truth!" Chad muttered.

"I'm not going to let these sleazy people get away with hurting you and ruining Graham's and Claudia's lives," Emma decided, "even if I actually have to call my father to back up the threat."

"Maybe it won't go that far," Carrie said.

"Let's ask Sam her opinion," Emma suggested.

"But you and Sam never agree about things like this," Carrie said with surprise.

"Sam's pragmatic," Emma said. "Sometimes I'm not. Have you seen her, by the way? I haven't caught a glimpse of her for hours."

"She ran by here just before you showed up, actually," Carrie said. "She seemed in a hurry to get somewhere."

"Hey, there, y'all!" Lorell drawled, sidling up to them on the deck. She attempted a smile, but she was feeling so horrible about

Flash's rejection that it was becoming hard for even her to fake it. "Isn't this boat sweet?" she chirped. "Of course, Daddy's is bigger," she added.

"Of course," Carrie echoed, rolling her eyes.

"Flash is on the lower deck takin' the most fabulous shots," Lorell continued. "I hate to disturb him when he's makin' great art."

"Gee, it seemed to me like he was more interested in making Emma," Chad joked.

Lorell pushed her hair back behind one ear and straightened her shoulders. "Where I come from, people are known by the company they keep," she told Chad. "Emma's friends are trash, so I guess you can figure out what that makes Emma. And Flash is not interested in trash."

Emma had to laugh at that one. "Gee, Carrie, I didn't know they were letting trash into Yale these days."

"Oh, not her," Lorell said. "She's merely boring. I meant the one who tried to sleep with my guy to get her modeling career started."

"Come on, Lorell," Carrie chided. "Even you don't believe that's true."

"Of course it's true," said Lorell, who by

this time had practically talked herself into believing Flash's version of what had happened. "She's a total slut. Just tonight she was throwin' herself at that Johnny Angel. He could hardly get away from her. His girlfriend told me she caught them together, with Sam half-naked, and Sam was just begging Johnny to do anything with her that he wanted."

"That's a vicious lie," Emma snapped.

"It's not a lie," Lorell insisted, "so you can wipe that smug look right off your face, Emma Cresswell."

Carrie and Emma looked at each other. They were both thinking the same thing.

"We've got to find Sam," Carrie said.

Emma nodded. "I'll see you later, okay?" she said to Chad.

"I'll help you look for her," he offered.

"No, but thanks anyway," Emma said.

"She went this way," Carrie said, pointing aft. Emma and Carrie hurried off.

Chad looked at Lorell. "Either you really, really care about this Flash guy, or you are the biggest bitch I ever met in my life."

"Both," Lorell said softly as she watched Carrie and Emma's retreating forms. She felt as if she'd won, but she couldn't figure out why she felt so terribly, terribly sad.

Carrie and Emma had looked everywhere, but couldn't find Sam. Finally they ran into Johnny at the bar and asked him if he'd seen her.

"Not for a while," he said. He looked down into his glass. "I think I really upset her. I didn't mean to—I think she's a great kid," he said earnestly.

"She's not a kid," Emma snapped.

"She's real young, is what I mean," Johnny explained. "I thought . . . well, never mind what I thought. I just didn't know everything was such a big deal to her until it was too late."

"Now I'm really worried," Emma said as she and Carrie hurried back up on deck.

"Let's go back in the same direction I saw her running," Carrie suggested. "She's got to be somewhere."

"You don't think she'd . . ." Emma began. What she was thinking was too horrible to say out loud.

"No," Carrie insisted. "She's upset, she's not suicidal."

They were far from the noise of the party, and they looked around them on the dimly lit deck, not knowing which way to go. Suddenly they both heard a noise. It sounded like someone shuddering, and then a sob. It seemed to be coming from somewhere right below them.

"Did you hear that?" Emma asked Carrie.

They both leaned over the rail, and looked down into a ten-foot dinghy, bobbing in the water. They could barely make out the outline of a figure who seemed to be huddled in the corner.

"Sam?" Carrie whispered as loudly as she could.

"Go away," came back Sam's tear-filled voice.

"Please come up," Emma said. "We'll go somewhere and talk."

"I don't want to talk," Sam said. "I want to die."

Emma waited only a second before she climbed over the rail and began making her way down the ladder that led to the dinghy.

"Is it safe?" Carrie called down to her.

"Of course," Emma said. "It's cleated to the yacht."

Carrie took the two cameras off her neck and carefully set them down on the deck, then followed Emma down the ladder into the darkness of the sea.

ELEVEN

"Are you okay?" Carrie asked, gingerly sitting down next to Sam in the small, rocking boat. Emma automatically sat opposite them to balance the dinghy.

"No," Sam said.

Carrie and Emma waited for Sam to elaborate, but she didn't. This was not a good sign. They'd never seen Sam depressed enough not to be funny, or sarcastic, or *something*.

"What happened?" Emma asked gently.

"I can't talk about it, it's too horrible," Sam cried.

"Wouldn't it make you feel better?" Carrie asked.

"Nothing would make me feel better except jumping into the water and never coming up for air," Sam said.

Carrie and Emma didn't say anything because they didn't know what to say. They didn't want to pry or to force Sam to talk. On the other hand, she was clearly miserable.

In the distance they could hear the sounds of the party—music, people laughing and having a wonderful, festive time. Someone turned the music up, and for a moment they could hear the final notes of "Breathless for You."

Hearing that song sent Sam over the edge. "Oh God, I hate myself!" she sobbed. "I wish I'd never met him!"

"Johnny?" Emma ventured.

"He's up there right now, laughing at me," Sam whispered.

"No," Carrie objected.

"It's true!" Sam cried tragically. "I made a total ass out of myself, and he's up there telling everyone about this stupid kid who threw herself at him."

"But you didn't!" Emma said. "I was with you at the cocktail party. I saw what happened. He pursued you, not the other way around."

"Yeah, like I had this big plan," Sam sniffed, "pretending not to be interested in him. He must have known all along. He must have thought I was just another bimbo groupie, throwing myself at him."

"No one could think that about you!" Carrie said fervently. "How can you even say that?"

"Because it's true," Sam said. "We were talking, and I thought we got really close after a while . . ." Sam gulped. It was hard to tell even her two best friends what a fool she'd been. "Anyway," she continued, "we started kissing, and he told me I was special, and I . . . I thought he meant it. Then we went to this bedroom, to be alone. I wanted to—it's not like he forced me. I had all these stupid dreams, like that he really cared for me, and that we'd become a couple, and that we understood each other because we're both dancers. . . ."

Carrie nodded, and she and Emma waited expectantly. Sam looked out into the water, as if she were looking at the rerun of a horrible movie she'd just lived through.

"So we were in this bedroom, and it was so romantic and everything, and then he took off my top and his T-shirt, and . . . I was going to do it, you know, I wanted to,

175

and then . . ." Sam's voice broke, but she forced herself to continue. "This girl, Linda, came into the room, and she said she's his girlfriend, and she stood there laughing at me."

"That's horrible!" Emma breathed. "How could he not tell you his girlfriend was here?"

"After he got her out of the room he told me they were just friends now." Sam gulped. "He was surprised that I was so upset. He said he thought I was just looking for some excitement. Yeah, good old Sam, out for some cheap thrills. It never meant anything to him at all!" she sobbed. "God, I want to die!"

Carrie reached out and put her hand on Sam's knee. "I'm so sorry."

"You shouldn't blame yourself, Sam," Emma said.

"Why not?" Sam cried. "It's all my fault!"

"But it's not!" Emma insisted. "So what if you dreamed about having a future with Johnny? I don't see what was so wrong with that!"

"Oh, sure," Sam sniffed. "Like Johnny Angel is going to fall in love with Samantha Bridges from Junction, Kansas."

"I think he'd be lucky to get you," Carrie said loyally.

"That's not real life," Sam said sadly. "Let's face it, I made the whole thing up. I built up this big fantasy in my head. Well, it's a joke, and the joke's on me."

"Stop knocking yourself!" Emma counseled. "Okay, maybe you did get a little carried away, but that doesn't mean it couldn't really happen!"

"Right!" Carrie agreed. "Look at Graham and Claudia! She used to be a secretary, and Graham fell in love with her. I like Claudia a lot, but she's not smarter or nicer or prettier than you are, you know."

"Maybe stuff like that happens," Sam allowed in a small voice, "but it's not going to happen to me. I pretend to be so hot, but all I am is a tall, skinny girl from a small town with big dreams that will never come true."

After Carrie and Emma left to find Sam, Chad talked with Lorell for a while. He was curious about her—could she possibly be for real? He liked to study people, because mostly that was what he painted. He stared at Lorell in the moonlight, wondering if it would be possible to capture the beauty of her perfect features and the bitchiness and insecurity behind them.

"I had my portrait done for my debutante party last year," Lorell said when Chad told her that he was an artist. "It's hanging over the fireplace in Daddy's den. Mama was jealous, to tell the truth, because her portrait used to hang there," Lorell added irrelevantly. She turned to face Chad. "Let me ask you a question," she said.

"Okay," Chad agreed.

"I hope you'll tell me the truth, because you don't know me and it's highly unlikely that we'll ever see each other again, don't you agree?" Lorell asked.

Chad nodded and leaned against the rail.

"Am I pretty?"

"You're good-looking," Chad answered. That was the truth. Feature for feature, it was hard to find a flaw. Yet it seemed to Chad that the ugliness of her character somehow came through and spoiled whatever actual prettiness was there.

"Do I have a good body?"

"You know you do," Chad answered.

"Better than Emma's?"

"Hey, this is a contest that I do not intend to judge," Chad said, holding up his hands as if to ward her off.

"I do, you know," Lorell said, stepping closer to Chad.

It was then that he smelled the liquor on her breath, and realized that she was not exactly sober.

"Maybe we should go back downstairs," Chad ventured.

"I bet I kiss better than she does," Lorell said. She took one more step toward Chad, and before he knew it Lorell had her lips planted on his in a one-sided, passionate kiss.

"Whoa, Lorell babe, keep up the floor show!" Flash boomed from somewhere behind them.

Lorell turned around. Chad felt horribly embarrassed and couldn't figure out how he had gotten himself into this situation, but Lorell looked smug and happy. That was when he realized that she had been hoping that Flash might catch them. It had worked out exactly as she had planned.

"Oh, hey there, Flash," Lorell drawled demurely. "We were just enjoyin' the moonlight."

"Looks like you were enjoying more than that, babe," Flash observed.

"It's really not how it looks—" Chad began.

"He couldn't keep his hands off me," Lorell interrupted. "He's an artist," she added, "and he wants to paint me."

"Hey, I never said—" Chad objected.

"Nude," Lorell continued. "He thinks I have a better body than Emma."

Flash laughed. "Lorell, babe, let's face it. The guy told you that because he's got a shot at getting you to drop your drawers, and no shot at getting the ice maiden to drop hers."

Chad moved between them. "Listen, I never—look, this has nothing to do with me, okay? So, um, I'll catch you later."

He started away from them quickly, but neither one of them noticed. They were too busy staring at each other.

"Emma Cresswell is probably frigid," Lorell said. "She probably doesn't even like men."

"What she is is a lady, babe, something you aren't too familiar with. Where is she, by the by? I was hoping to get a few more shots of her tonight. I think she could do big

180

things as a petite model, and I'm just the guy to do it."

Tears came to Lorell's eyes. "How . . . how can you be so stuck on her, and treat me so badly?" she whispered. "I just don't understand."

"Because I'm a schmuck," Flash said good-naturedly.

"But I love you," Lorell said. "Doesn't that mean anything to you?"

"This is not a subject I'm real comfortable with," Flash admitted. "How about we go back down and party, have a few laughs—"

"I'm talkin' about love, Fred," Lorell said, deliberately calling Flash by his real name. "I've stood by you, and helped you, and defended you. I paid for your new equipment because I believe in you as an artist. And then you treat me like dirt!"

Flash was silent for a moment. "So let me ask you, why do you allow yourself to be treated that way?"

"Because I love you!" Lorell cried.

"You don't love me," Flash said quietly. "I don't know what it is. Maybe you love the idea of being with a guy your parents hate so much. But no way can you love a guy who treats you as badly as I treat you."

"Then why do you do it?" Lorell asked.

Flash fiddled with one of the gold chains around his neck. "It's part of the whole thing between us, babe. I treat you crappy, and you take it. If I treated you great, you'd drop me like a hot potato."

"That's not true," Lorell objected.

"Yes it is," Flash insisted. "I'd be just another poor schmuck who treats you great, and you'd walk all over me. Well, sorry, princess. Nobody walks all over the Flashman."

"Why can't you believe that I actually, really love you?" Lorell cried.

"Because no one ever has," Flash said honestly.

"I can make it up to you, if you'll just let me," Lorell began, opening her arms to embrace Flash.

"No can do, babe," Flash said, stepping away from her. He was embarrassed that for just a moment he'd actually spoken honestly, from his heart. It was dangerous territory—who knew where it could lead?

"Emma doesn't care anything about you!" Lorell cried. "You disgust her! She thinks you're a big joke!"

Flash gave Lorell a sad, crooked smile. "Hey, like Groucho Marx said, babe, I'd never belong to any club that would have me as a member. Ciao, babe. Gotta boogie!"

Flash left Lorell standing there by herself on the deck. Tears rolled silently down her cheeks as she watched the first guy she had ever loved turn his back on her and walk away.

How can this be happening to me, Lorell Courtland? she thought desperately. *It has to be someone's fault, and it certainly isn't mine! It has to be Emma's fault, that's it! Nothing ever gets to Emma. She's always been the perfect lady. She probably doesn't even go to the bathroom, or have to wax her bikini line,* Lorell thought despondently. *And she never, ever brags about her money, or feels desperate for people to like her. It just isn't fair!*

Lorell wandered toward the rear of the yacht, her heart breaking and vicious thoughts about Emma dancing through her mind. She leaned against the rail and looked up at the stars. Suddenly, out of nowhere, she saw a shooting star, and she quickly made a wish. *Let Flash love me, and let him want me more than he wants Emma Cress-well*, she wished, closing her eyes tightly.

Just then she thought she heard the sound of voices coming from below her. She listened carefully. It sounded like Emma's voice.

"You can't let him break your heart!" she heard the voice say. It definitely belonged to Emma. Lorell would know that perfect, highbrow Boston accent anywhere.

Lorell peered down into the darkness. It took a moment for her eyes to adjust, and then she saw them. Sam, Carrie, and Emma were sitting in a small dinghy that was attached to the back of the yacht. Their voices were soft and earnest.

Now Lorell was sorry she had wasted her wish, because what she wanted to wish instead was that that little boat would just drift off to sea with Emma on board. Surely if Flash had a chance to be alone with Lorell, if Emma was nowhere in the vicinity, he'd appreciate her again. Besides, Emma would deserve it. And even *she* wouldn't look so cool and perfect anymore stuck in a dinghy at sea.

Her eyes lit on the iron cleat mooring the small boat to the yacht. It wouldn't be difficult to slip the cleat, setting the dinghy adrift.

Lorell's heart hammered in her chest. Could she really dare to do it? Yes. She made up her plan as she crept stealthily toward the cleat. Probably no one would miss the girls or the dinghy for a while. Everyone was too busy partying. Lorell would get to be alone with Flash, which would change everything. The weather was calm, so the girls wouldn't really get hurt, even if they did get a little scared, Lorell rationalized. And she would certainly call the Coast Guard eventually, after she "discovered" that the dinghy and the girls were missing. Everyone would say she was a hero, for saving their lives, and surely Flash would have to love her then.

"I'll never live this down. Never," Lorell heard Sam sob. She could barely make out the silhouettes of Emma and Carrie, who were murmuring comforting words to their friend. None of them was paying any attention to anything going on aboard the yacht. Slowly Lorell reached out her hand and unhooked the cleat. The rope came off easily. She held her breath for a moment, wondering if the girls would notice that they'd been set adrift and were floating away from the yacht.

But they were too busy discussing Sam's dilemma to realize anything was amiss. The small boat they were on was now all that stood between them and the bottomless, inky depths of the sea.

TWELVE

"One thing I know for sure," Sam said, "I can never face Johnny again. I'd be completely mortified."

"He wasn't such a prince, you know," Emma said. "I think he really took advantage of the situation."

"Oh, Emma, rock stars aren't like ordinary people. They don't have to follow the rules that everyone else follows," Sam told her. "They're like—oh, I don't know. Like royalty or something."

"Only if you give them that kind of power," Emma declared firmly.

Sam sighed. "You don't understand because you've been treated like royalty all your life." She looked at Carrie in the darkness. "Didn't you fall for Billy partly because he's the lead singer of the Flirts?" Sam asked. "You told me yourself you couldn't believe that a rock star like Billy, who could get any girl he wanted, actually wanted you."

"I admit it," Carrie said. "But look at all the trouble I got into when I tried to be what I thought Billy wanted me to be. I changed everything about myself—my looks, my personality, everything—just to try and get him to like me. Well, it turned out that he liked me for who I actually was, not for who I was pretending to be. The only person who ended up not liking me was me."

"Nice speech, Car," Sam said, resting her chin on her cupped hands. "But I didn't see him jumping through any hoops for you. No, he had the power, because he's a rock star. It changes everything."

"That's silly," Emma objected.

"You think so?" Sam asked. "Tell that to the thousands of girls who would do just about anything to get a famous rock musician."

"I'm just saying you're worth more than that," Carrie said gently.

"Besides, it's not like you really know Johnny," Emma pointed out. "You just met him today."

"But everything seemed so perfect," Sam sighed. "I've run the conversations we had over and over in my mind, to see where I went wrong. . . ."

"But you didn't go wrong!" Emma insisted. "That's what I'm trying to tell you. You didn't give him a chance to get to know you. You were too busy playing a game, working out some complex scheme to get him!"

Sam didn't say anything for a moment. She trailed her fingers over the edge of the dinghy. "I hate it when you're right," she finally muttered.

"You just don't give yourself enough credit," Carrie said softly. "I bet if Johnny Angel had a chance to get to know you, then he really *would* fall for you!"

"Yeah, sure," Sam snorted. "He'd probably turn down, say, Julia Roberts if I was to give him the nod."

"Fame and money aren't everything," Emma said.

"You're right," Sam agreed. "A great set of lungs helps, too, and I haven't got that, either!" As dark as it was on the dinghy, Sam could still make out the grave expressions on her friends' faces. Suddenly she had to laugh at herself. "Pity party!" she screamed. "What do you hate most about yourself?"

"My thighs!" Carrie yelled, quickly picking up on Sam's mood change.

"Emma?" Sam prodded her.

"Uh . . . uh . . ." Emma stammered.

"Oh, come on," Sam chided her, "even *you* must hate something about yourself."

"My mother!" Emma blurted out.

"Being from Kansas!" Sam yelled.

"Having to be perfect!" Carrie screamed.

"Being short!" yelled Emma.

"Being a virgin!" Sam groaned.

"*Not* being a virgin!" Carrie groaned even louder.

"Being a spoiled, rich, worthless princess with an empty, meaningless life!" Emma screamed loudest of all.

Sam and Carrie stared at her. "Is that what you really think?" Carrie asked.

"No, no, not really," Emma stammered.

"Yes, it is," Sam said wonderingly. "That really is what you think, isn't it? And here I've always thought that your life is so perfect and everything."

"Well, it's not," Emma said quietly.

"Everyone's got problems," Carrie said.

"My grandmother used to tell me that if you took all your problems and put them into a brown paper bag, and threw that bag into the middle of a room with everyone else's problems, and you could see what was inside each bag, you'd want your own bag back," Sam said.

"Do you believe that?" Carrie asked.

Sam thought a minute. "Hell, no!"

All three of them had to laugh at that. Suddenly the whole day struck them as having been utterly absurd, and they laughed so hard they had to hold their stomachs. That started the boat rocking, which made them shriek and laugh even harder.

"Come on, you guys, I get seasick really easily," Sam protested between peals of laughter.

"Which is another thing she hates about herself!" Carrie yelped. That started them all laughing again, which made the dinghy rock even more.

"Hey, this kind of dinghy was not meant for rock and roll!" Emma objected good-naturedly. "Especially if the weight isn't balanced."

"Since I'm sure I, unfortunately, weigh

the most, I can fix that," Carrie said, getting up to move to the center of the boat.

"Careful!" Emma cautioned her. She reached out a hand to steady Carrie, but Carrie didn't take it.

"Oh no!" Carrie whispered, frozen in a half-crouch in the center of the boat. Her eyes were riveted in the direction of the yacht. Only the yacht wasn't there.

Sam and Emma's eyes followed Carrie's to where the yacht should have been.

"We came unhooked!" Sam screamed, grabbing the edge of the dinghy.

All three of them looked frantically around them, but there was nothing to see except an endless black ocean.

"Hey! Hey! We're here! We're here!" Sam yelled, attempting to stand up in the boat.

"Sit down!" Emma commanded her. "All you'll do is capsize us. Nobody can possibly hear you."

"How could this have happened?" Carrie whispered.

No one answered. For a moment all three of them were silent as their predicament fully sank into their minds.

"They'll realize right away that we're gone, don't you think?" Sam asked anxiously. "And they'll come looking for us, and then they'll realize the dinghy is gone. . . ." Her voice trailed off. Even she wasn't convinced that would happen anytime soon.

"Sure," Carrie finally agreed, trying to sound positive. "Meanwhile, as long as we sit still nothing can happen to us, right?"

Both Sam and Carrie were looking at Emma, since she was the only one who seemed to know something about boats and the sea. Emma didn't answer. She knew just enough to know exactly what kind of danger they could really be in, and she didn't want to scare them any more than they already were.

"Look around and see what's in the boat," Emma suggested. "Maybe there's a flare we can shoot off or something."

Sam quickly slid to the far edge of her seat and looked around.

"Careful!" Emma cautioned her. "Don't make any sudden movements or shift your weight around like that!"

"There's a knife here," Carrie said, gingerly picking up a small leather case. She drew the knife out. It had a blade of about three inches that glinted in the moonlight.

"That could be useful," Emma said, looking around her.

"For what?" Sam said nervously. "Skinning fish? I don't even eat sushi in Japanese restaurants!"

"There's a metal box under there," Carrie said, pointing in Emma's direction.

Emma pulled it out from under her seat. "A first-aid kit," she told them. "And there's a chocolate bar in here—although it looks like it's from the year one."

"I'm sure we won't be here long enough to actually get hungry," Carrie said.

"I get hungry just thinking about getting hungry," Sam said, biting her lower lip.

"Hey, a sail!" Emma cried. She had opened a long nylon bag that had been half-hidden in the dark recesses of the dinghy. "If we put up the sail, it will help give us some control over the dinghy," Emma explained, "and it will also make it easier for someone to see us." She carefully started to pull the sail out of the bag. "Grab that end," she told Carrie, "but try not to shift your weight too much."

Carrie grabbed one end of the sail and Emma grabbed the other. The sail was already attached to a makeshift mast that was designed to fit into a holder in the floor of the dinghy.

"Lower it into there," Emma instructed Carrie.

Carefully the two girls lowered the mast into the holder. The sail immediately started to flap wildly.

"It's out of control!" Sam screamed, clutching the sides of the dinghy as the boat rocked wildly.

"Don't panic!" Emma yelled. "It's okay. Just don't move! Keep your weight centered in the boat!" Emma felt under her seat for the small rudder she had seen there, and pulled it out. "Just hold on, everything is okay!" she called to Sam. The sail was making a ton of noise as it flapped crazily above them. Even Carrie looked ready to faint or cry.

Emma attached the rudder to the back of the boat. "When I pull on the sheet we'll be okay," she yelled. She pulled on the rope, attached to the far end of the sail, and quickly the sail filled with wind and stopped flapping out of control. Emma heaved a sigh of relief.

"How did you do that?" Sam asked in awe.

"I just put the sail up, and pulled the sheet

tight—the sheet is the rope that controls the sail," Emma explained.

"I think she means how did you know how to do it?" Carrie asked in a tremulous voice.

"I've put up sails before," Emma said. "My dad taught me."

"Thank God for that," Carrie said. "I was petrified!"

"We should be okay now," Emma said, "as long as we don't do anything stupid."

They were all quiet for a moment, letting their heartbeats return to normal.

"This is my fault," Sam finally whispered.

"It's not your fault unless you unhooked the cleat from the yacht," Carrie pointed out.

"You know what I mean," Sam said. "You guys crawled down here to help me. If I hadn't made such an ass out of myself with Johnny, and if I hadn't wanted to escape from the yacht—"

"And if wishes were horses, beggars would ride," Emma said irritably. "Just forget it. It's not your fault."

"Now you're ticked at me," Sam said. "I can tell. God, how could I have been such an idiot? How could I—"

"I, I, I!" Emma snapped. "Me, me, me!

196

Even in a disaster, you have to make your-self the center of attention!"

"Wow, you must really hate me," Sam said in a small voice.

"I don't," Emma sighed. "I'm just . . . I'm just blowing off steam because I'm scared."

"You did great so far," Carrie pointed out to Emma in a soft voice. "Sam and I would never have known to put up a sail."

"Yeah, we're depending on you," Sam said in a scared voice. "So please don't be mad at me now. You can be mad at me all you want once we get out of this, I promise. Just tell me it's okay for now," she pleaded.

Emma didn't answer. She really was frightened. And what scared her the most was that she was the only one who knew anything about how to save or protect them. It was all on her shoulders.

Nothing had ever been all on Emma's shoulders, and she didn't like the feeling. She looked vaguely in the sky for the North Star. She didn't even know which direction to sail in. She had never been out at night before. She couldn't buy her way out, or use her family's influence, or hire someone to do it for her. *But this is what you wanted,*

Emma reminded herself. *To be just like any ordinary eighteen-year-old.* She and her friends had no one to rely on but her, and she could mean the difference between life and death.

THIRTEEN

"What time is it, do you think?" Sam asked. Her teeth were chattering from the cold, but she didn't want to complain. It wasn't as if there was anything anyone could do about it.

"I don't know," Carrie said. "Maybe three or four. It seems like we've been out here forever." She tried to get the moonlight to catch the hands on her watch, but there wasn't enough light to see the time. "It's freezing," she added, briskly rubbing her hands over her arms.

"If you keep your body wrapped around itself, you'll stay warmer," Emma said.

"Daylight can't be that far away," Sam said. "Everything will be better once it's light."

"Right," Carrie agreed. "It's the dark that makes everything so scary."

Emma didn't say anything. She was thinking about the new problems the light could bring: the unrelenting sun beating down on their exposed skin, thirst that couldn't be slacked. Emma knew they couldn't live very long without fresh water. *But we can't possibly get stuck out here for that long*, Emma told herself. *Surely we'll be saved before things get critical.* If she kept telling herself that, she reasoned, maybe she'd start to believe it.

"Maybe if we sleep for a while the time will go faster," Sam suggested.

"No!" Emma snapped. "We can't fall asleep. We have to stay alert. It's dangerous to sleep."

The wind blew Sam's hair into her face, and she pushed it out of her eyes. She didn't want to ask Emma why it was dangerous because she didn't want to hear the dangers enumerated out loud. She just held herself tighter and looked up at the stars. That was when she realized there weren't any. And the wind that had come up suddenly was whipping her hair back into her face.

"It's getting kind of windy, isn't it?" Carrie ventured.

The sail was puffed out with the force of the air rushing into it. The previously calm sea was starting to ripple with waves, and the boat had begun to rock.

"Emma?" Sam asked. She didn't know what she was asking, but she needed some words of confidence.

"We're okay," Emma said, not knowing if they were okay at all. "It might just be some wind."

"I can't see the stars anymore," Sam whispered. "Before I could see zillions of them."

"Just clouds," Carrie said. "Right, Emma?"

The wind picked up, pushing into the sail. The boat traveled speedily through the black water, which was starting to churn around them.

"Oh, God," Sam breathed as they heard a clap of thunder in the distance. It was followed by a streak of lightning that lit up the boat. For the briefest of moments they could see the fear etched on one another's faces.

"Emma, what should we do?" Carrie asked in a frightened voice.

"I don't know!" Emma cried. "What makes you think I know?"

The rain started falling then, softly at first. Suddenly it seemed as if the sky had opened up. Lightning sizzled over their heads, followed closely by violent claps of thunder that burst through the skies.

The sail took the wind even more strongly then, forcing the boat to race swiftly over the water. Waves came up, splashing water into the boat, which rocked crazily and threatened to tip at any moment.

"Oh, my stomach," Sam moaned.

"She's seasick," Carrie cried, holding Sam's arms as she leaned over the side and retched.

"We've got to take the sail down!" Emma screamed over the noise of the storm. "It'll capsize us!" She let the sheet go, which started the sail flapping wildly. For a moment it seemed as if they were totally out of control. "Help me!" she yelled to Carrie, who was closest to her. Together they lifted the mast out of the holder and wrestled the sail down into the boat.

"We're going to sink!" Sam screamed. The boat was rapidly filling up with water.

Emma grabbed the first-aid kit and dumped out its contents. Quickly she started bailing water out of the boat with the metal box.

Sam looked around frantically for something to bail with, and found a rusty cup under the seat. Carrie was forced to use her hands, cupping them and pouring water off the side of the boat.

Among the three of them they were able to keep the boat from sinking. But the wind roared ever more fiercely, whipping sheets of rain against their frightened faces. Now the boat headed into the waves, rolling and pitching until the waves seemed as if they would crash over them and crush them into nothingness.

"Oh, God, please help us!" Sam screamed.

"Just keep bailing!" Carrie yelled.

Emma bailed frantically from her end of the boat. They were rolling sickeningly with the waves, and she felt as if she might be seasick, too. "We're okay! We'll be okay!" she yelled. But she didn't really believe it. A wave that seemed fifty feet high washed over them, and they just barely managed to stay afloat. Sam was sick again. No matter what they did, Emma knew, the dinghy could only take so much more of this pounding. There was nothing they could do, nowhere to turn, no way for them to save themselves.

A huge bolt of lightning lit up the sky, and Emma caught a glimpse of what looked like a mass of something ahead of them in the water. She peered into the darkness, and another bolt of lightning flashed like a neon light. Some wreckage? A reef? Maybe there was one crazy chance to save them . . .

"Grab the sail!" Emma screamed at Carrie, who could barely make out what Emma was saying over the cacophony of the storm. But in the light from the next bolt of lightning Carrie saw Emma struggling with the sail, and she helped her lift it. Emma quickly knotted the rope that had been attached to the yacht around the sail.

They held it for a moment, and then the sky lit up again.

"Now! Drop it!" Emma screamed. She and Carrie dropped the sail into the water. There was a tugging sensation, and then although the boat was still being thrown around by the waves, it seemed moored, held fast in one place.

"What did you do?" Sam yelled as she bailed frantically with her cup.

"We're anchored to a reef or something!" Emma yelled.

The noise of the storm made it too difficult to speak. The girls just bailed and held on to the boat.

After what seemed like forever, but was probably only a half-hour or so, the rain seemed to slacken a bit and the wind died down somewhat.

"I think it's stopping," Sam said tremulously.

"Just keeping bailing," Emma instructed.

They worked in silence for a while, praying that the worst of the storm really was over. The rain slowed to a drizzle, and then finally it stopped. The dinghy bobbed, but it no longer seemed ready to turn over at any moment.

"What did you do?" Sam asked in a hushed voice.

"We threw the sail overboard and it caught on something," Emma said. "It's working like an anchor, so the boat can't move around very much."

"How did you know to do that?" Sam asked.

"I didn't," Emma answered honestly. "I mean, it just came into my head when I saw this dark shape lit up by the lightning."

"Do you think we'll be okay now?" Sam asked, her voice faltering.

"We'll be okay," said Carrie reassuringly. "Look, the stars are coming out again."

The girls all looked up at the sky, which yawned hugely above them. They were soaking wet, shivering, cold, and very happy to be alive.

Carrie closed her eyes and started to pray silently that God would let them come through this. Sam started to cry, the tears mingling with the rain and sea water on her frightened face. Emma kept looking around her, staying ever alert to any new dangers.

"This doesn't seem real, does it?" Sam said in a soft voice.

"I know," Carrie agreed. "I feel like I must be stuck in a nightmare, and I can't wake up."

"I was just thinking about my family," Sam said with chattering teeth. "I hope we get rescued before anyone calls them. They'd be so scared."

"Mine, too," Carrie said. "Now I can't

believe I ever wanted to spend Christmas away from them."

"My sister, Ruth Ann, makes these great Christmas cookies," Sam said. "They're shaped like stars. And she always gives me a present from this sexy lingerie catalogue. She saves up and then sends away for something for me. It's funny, because Ruth Ann is younger than I am and wouldn't be caught dead in stuff like that anyway. It's just something she does for me every Christmas."

"We always sing Christmas carols," Carrie said wistfully. "I stand near my dad, and we sing harmonies. He's always a little flat, and I always tease him."

A tear worked its way down Emma's cheek. She had no happy family Christmas memories. She searched her mind for any happy family memories at all, and all she came up with was the summer when her father had taught her to sail.

"I should have talked to Mom and Dad before I just dropped out of school," Sam said. "I should have considered their feelings. God, I can be such a selfish snot sometimes. . . ."

"I was just thinking about Josh," Carrie said, "and all the great Christmases we've had together. It's funny—I haven't thought about Billy at all. I think if something happened, it would be Josh I would really miss."

"Maybe that's who you really love," Emma said. "Maybe Billy's just an infatuation."

"I don't know," said Carrie. "Billy's a fantastic guy. Maybe we just haven't had enough time to really get to know each other yet."

"I've never been in love," Sam said, "and that's the truth. I don't even think I know what it is. Maybe I'm just not capable of it."

"Of course you are," Carrie said.

"I think you'd fall in love if you stopped playing games with guys," Emma said, still constantly looking around them alertly, "and if you'd let them really get to know you."

"*I* don't even know me, so how could they?" Sam asked. She shivered and wrapped her arms more tightly around herself. "I'm very, very scared," she said in a tiny voice.

"Have you ever been in love, Em?" Carrie asked, hoping to stay off the topic of how scared they all were.

"I love Kurt," Emma confessed. "Even after everything that happened last summer."

"But you broke up with him," Sam reminded her.

"I know," Emma said. "Everything got so messed up between us. But I just can't forget him. He's the first guy who ever really saw the me I'd like to be, instead of just the me I am."

As Emma stared out at the sea she thought about the night she and Kurt had walked on the beach, when she'd confessed to him her secret desire to join the Peace Corps, perhaps even go to Africa. She told him she wanted to do something important in her life. Instead of thinking that that was a crazy ambition for a pampered rich girl, he had encouraged her. The greatest gift he'd given her had been his belief that she was a person with enough guts and backbone to actually do what she wanted to do. Emma sighed. The problem was that *she* didn't believe she had the strength and courage to do it. Being with Chad had just reminded her of that.

"What's that?" Sam shrieked, pointing at a large mass moving swiftly toward them in

209

the water. By the light from the moon they could make out what looked like a fin swishing toward them, heading right for their dinghy.

"It looks like a shark!" Carrie cried. "Oh, please, don't let this be happening!"

"Sam, give me that knife you found," Emma instructed tersely.

Sam passed the knife, which Emma unsheathed and held poised over the side of the boat.

"Sharks don't necessarily attack," Emma said in a tight voice. "A lot of them live near reefs and never bother anyone."

"Right," Carrie agreed, clearly frightened out of her mind. She clutched the sides of the dinghy until her knuckles turned white. "I read that somewhere. Unless they smell blood."

The shark was circling them now. The three girls sat rigid, afraid to move or breathe, terrified of attracting the wrath of the killer beast that swam around them.

"I read that you have to hit them in the snout." Carrie's voice trembled. "There's a certain spot—"

"It's the most sensitive spot on a shark's

body," Sam said nervously. "I remember seeing it on a National Geographic special or something. Their skin is like leather everywhere else. Hitting it in the snout is probably the only way we can hurt it."

"Or just make it angry enough to attack us," Carrie added, her voice shaking.

"It probably doesn't want us," Emma said tremulously, trying to reassure herself as well as her friends. "Maybe some fish got injured on the reef or whatever it is during the storm, and it smells that." Emma sat stock-still, her knife poised over the water.

"Don't make it mad!" Sam pleaded.

"I won't make a move if it doesn't," Emma said through clenched teeth.

They held their breath as the shark circled them once more, and then as quickly as it had arrived it was gone.

Carrie took a deep gulp of air. "I think it's gone. Thank you," she added in a whisper, her eyes closed.

"It could come back," Emma said. "We have to stay alert."

They waited and watched silently. There was no way to tell how much time had passed. Finally, Sam noticed a light on the horizon.

"I think dawn's coming," she said in a hushed voice.

As they sat there, huddled in their freezing, wet clothes, the sky began to lighten.

"Someone will find us now," Carrie said quietly. "I know they will."

"We've been missing for hours," Sam added. "The Coast Guard will be looking."

"I'm sure it won't be long," Emma agreed. Her voice sounded much more confident than she was, however. Of the three of them, only she realized how vast the ocean really was, and how far they might be from the point at which they had begun. It was sort of like looking for a needle in a haystack.

"I can't believe that just a few hours ago I was crying over Johnny Angel," Sam said. "He seems so unimportant now."

"Lots of things seem unimportant now," Carrie said. "And lots of other things seem more important."

"Yeah," Sam agreed. "Like my parents, like even my stupid sister."

"Like my photography," Carrie said. "Like how much I was worried about what Faith would do about the pictures of Graham. It's not as though it's my life's ambition to be a rock-and-roll photographer. It's just something I got lucky and fell into, you know?" she said to her friends.

They nodded. It was true. Carrie hadn't even listened to much rock music before becoming Graham and Claudia's au pair. She really preferred jazz.

"I want to do documentary stuff, you know, photojournalism about things that are important, that mean something," Carrie said earnestly. "Faith O'Connor can't really hurt me."

"What about what she's doing to Graham?" Emma asked.

"That's more complicated," Carrie admitted. "I think Faith is totally wrong to do what she's doing, but I can't make everything okay. I always try to make everything okay for everybody—with my family, with my friends. It's exhausting!"

"If we get saved—" Sam began.

"*When* we get saved," Carrie said firmly.

"When we get saved," Sam corrected herself, "I'm going to call and tell my parents I love them."

"And I'm going to talk to Graham myself,

instead of trying to manipulate a situation that belongs to him and not to me," Carrie promised.

"And another thing," Sam said. "I'm going to quit putting my energy into trying to get a guy just because he's a hot, successful dancer or singer. I'd rather put the energy into turning *myself* into a hot, successful dancer or singer!"

"Great idea," said Emma. "But do you think you could concentrate on dance? I don't think singing is your strong suit."

"I just need more practice," Sam said with dignity. "Anyhow, I don't hear you making any plans. What are you going to do when we get back?" she asked Emma.

"I don't know," Emma said bitterly. "Maybe I'll call my father and ask him to introduce me to the twenty-three-year-old girl he's engaged to."

"Maybe you could finally apply to the Peace Corps," Carrie suggested.

"It's a ridiculous idea," Emma said. "I could never really do it."

"Why not, if it's what you really want?" Carrie asked.

"Because . . . because . . . " Emma hesitated.

"Because you're a spoiled rich girl who has to sleep on monogrammed sheets, maybe?" Sam asked.

"I'm not!" Emma protested.

"Oh, come on," Sam said dismissively. "You could never cut it. Why don't you just ease your conscience by making a fat donation and then jet off to the Riviera to soothe your nerves?"

"Sam!" Carrie cried. "That's so mean!"

"I'm not like that!" Emma yelled. "Who do you think just saved us in that storm? *I* did! *I* was the one who knew what to do, and *I* was the one who did it! *Me!*"

Sam and Carrie sat silently, staring at Emma.

"That's right, Em," Sam finally said in a gentler voice. "It took you long enough to realize it. If we come through this," she continued, "it'll be because of you. You're capable of doing anything you set your mind to, including building mud huts in Africa, if that's what you want to do."

Carrie shot Sam a look of admiration. She hadn't known her friend had it in her to be so perceptive.

"You . . . you really think . . ." Emma faltered.

"Oh, yes!" Carrie cried, agreeing with Sam. "I know we always feel like we're going to live forever, but we're not! If you don't do what's really important to you, what's in your heart, then you're just wasting your life!"

"I don't want to waste my life," Emma said in a hushed voice, hugging herself for warmth. "I really don't."

"Look!" Sam cried, pointing to the horizon off the left side of the dinghy. "Do you see something?"

"I think it's a boat!" Carrie called. "We're going to be saved!"

Emma squinted into the distance. "It's coming toward us," she said with relief. "They'll have to see us."

They watched eagerly as the large vessel swiftly came toward them.

"It's the Coast Guard!" Emma cried eagerly. "I recognize the markings on the boat!"

"Hey! We're here! We're here!" Sam yelled, waving frantically.

Carrie and Emma joined in waving,

laughing and crying all at once, knowing their ordeal was about to end.

"This is the United States Coast Guard," they heard a male voice boom through a loudspeaker. "We are prepared to take you aboard."

FOURTEEN

"Excuse me, ladies," said Lieutenant Chip Sallinger as he approached the girls down in the galley. The tall, muscular, tow-headed officer had been put in charge of them while they were on the ship. He'd done an excellent job, too. First it had been established that nothing was physically wrong with any of them due to their ordeal. After they had taken hot showers, Chip had gotten them clean, dry shirts and pants, and had made them a pot of steaming hot coffee. He'd also brought them some fresh squeezed orange juice, which they'd guzzled thirstily.

"Captain Pennell told me to tell you that he just received a ship-to-ship communication from the *Vestal Virgin*. Your friends are docked and waiting for you."

"Thanks," Sam said, giving him a wide

grin. Carrie and Emma smiled, too. They were safe at last.

Chip smiled back. Sam looked awfully cute in her oversized Coast Guard uniform, Carrie noted. "Can I get you anything else?" he asked them.

"No, we're fine," Carrie assured him.

"We'll be pulling up to your friends' yacht shortly," Chip said. "If you'd like to come up on deck, you can watch us approach."

They downed the rest of their coffee and scrambled up the steps just as the *Vestal Virgin* was coming into view.

"Look! There's tons of people up on deck waving at us!" Sam said excitedly. "Hiiiii!" she called, waving back happily. Even knowing that she wasn't close enough for anyone to hear her didn't curb her exuberance.

"I can't wait to step onto land," Carrie said. "I feel like I'm still rocking in that little dinghy."

"That'll stop after a while," Emma assured her.

Sam stopped waving and turned to her friends. "Hey, do you think Johnny Angel is still on the yacht? I absolutely do not want him to see me looking like this."

"What happened to how you were going to stop putting your energy into chasing after cool, successful guys and put your energy into becoming successful yourself?" Carrie asked.

"Did I say that?" Sam asked innocently. "I don't remember saying that. Does my hair look stringy?"

"Well, I remember what *I* said," Carrie emphasized. "I'm going to talk to Graham about what's going on, and beyond that, let the chips fall where they may. Faith can do whatever she wants, and so can Flash."

"So you don't want me to talk to Flash?" Emma said. "He really is scared of me, you know. I could get him to—"

"I don't want you to do anything," Carrie said firmly. "I mean, I appreciate your offer," she added hastily.

"It must be great to come from a family with that much wealth and power," Sam said wistfully.

"And easy to fall back on it," Carrie said.

"Hey!" Emma objected. "I never do that."

"No, you don't usually," Carrie agreed. "That's true. But it's always there, and it changes everything—even how you feel about yourself. If it weren't for that, I bet you already would have applied to the Peace Corps."

"Yeah, you're afraid you can't cut it on your own," Sam said.

"But you really can, Em," Carrie said fervently. "I know you can."

"We might not even be alive right now if it weren't for you," Sam said. "It wasn't as if you could pick up the phone and call your daddy to save you. You saved yourself. You saved *us*."

"I did, didn't I?" Emma marveled. "Maybe I really could . . ."

"Of course you really could!" Sam exclaimed. "Although I have to say that I think for you to be perfect-looking, *and* filthy rich, *and* a person as cool as you are is really nauseating."

"This is Captain Wayne Pennell of the United States Coast Guard," came the captain's voice over the loudspeaker. "We have three young ladies here who would like permission to board the *Vestal Virgin*."

"Permission to come aboard granted," came the answer.

A gangway was lowered to the *Vestal Virgin*.

"Thank you so much," Carrie said, shaking the captain's hand. All three girls crowded around.

"Saying that seems inadequate," Emma said.

"Ten thousand thank-yous," Sam said. "My future children-that-I'm-not-sure-I'll-ever-have thank you."

The captain smiled. "Just doing my job, ladies," he said. "But it happens to be a part of my job that is very rewarding. I wish you wonderful lives."

Sam waved to Chip, who gave her a thumbs-up sign and then waved back. Finally, they crossed the gangway to the *Vestal Virgin*.

It seemed that just about everyone was still aboard and was hugging them and laughing and talking all at once.

"Thank God!" Graham and Claudia just kept saying as they hugged the girls.

Somehow the story got pieced together. Around two o'clock Johnny had gone looking for Sam. He had really wanted to apologize again to her, but he couldn't find her. Then Chad had mentioned that Emma had never come back after she'd run off with Carrie to find Sam. The two of them had alerted the captain. A thorough search of the yacht had been conducted, but it had been Lorell who had "noticed" that the dinghy was missing. That was when they had called the Coast Guard.

"What were you doing in that dinghy in the first place, and how did it come untied from the yacht?" Faith, always the reporter, asked.

"It just seemed like a good, private place to talk," Carrie said, covering for Sam. She was surprised to see that Faith was still there. "As for how we got loose from the yacht, it's a mystery."

"Yeah, one minute the ship was there, and the next minute it wasn't!" Sam said.

"I checked the cleat," the captain said. "There's no way it could just come untied. I take a lot of pride in the maintenance of this vessel."

"So how could it have happened, then?" Chad asked.

"As I said earlier," Captain Randall said stiffly, "someone had to have slipped the cleat. There's no other way to free the dinghy."

"Look, that's ridiculous," Graham said. "No one at my party would do that. I don't know what happened, and I don't care. I'm just glad that everyone is okay."

"No lawsuit?" Faith asked. "It might make a good story."

Graham ignored her and hugged Carrie again. "You had me really scared, girl."

Carrie hugged him back. "I'm fine now," she assured him. "Do you think . . . could I talk to you for a minute—privately?"

"Sure," he said, putting an arm around her shoulders. They headed to the other side of the deck.

"Sammi!" Lorell trilled, coming up and hugging a startled Sam. "I was so worried about ya'll!"

"I bet," said Sam, extricating herself from Lorell's embrace.

"But I was!" she protested loudly. "You can ask anyone!"

"Spare me," Sam muttered.

"Well!" Lorell sputtered. "That's the thanks I get for bein' so concerned!"

Flash came up next to her. "What did I miss? I was in the head," he said as he finished adjusting the zipper on his pants. "Oh, Big Red, you seem to have survived," he said, looking her over. Sam moved quickly to the other side of the deck. Then

Flash's eyes lit on Emma. "You too, princess. You look cute in that uniform —sort of a sexy, sailor-girl type thing, know what I mean?"

"Flash," Emma said frostily, "isn't it patently clear to you by now that I don't find you funny or amusing, that in fact I loathe you?" Emma's voice could have cut glass. She sounded exactly like her mother.

Flash blanched and attempted a smile. "Hey, babe, we're just doing that sparring thing, you know, like friends do."

"We aren't friends," Emma said. "I think you're an idiot."

"Don't you dare talk to my man that way!" Lorell threatened, stepping in front of Flash.

"Shut up, Lorell. You're boring me," Flash said loudly, trying to cover his embarrassment over what Emma had said to him. He adjusted the chains around his neck. "Get the equipment," he ordered Lorell. "We're outta here."

Lorell struggled not to let Flash's words make her cry. Instead, she turned her anger back toward Emma. "You ungrateful bitch!" she screamed. "*I* was the one who noticed the dinghy missing! You should be thanking

225

me! I could have let you drown, but I didn't!"

A thought occurred to Emma, and her eyes narrowed. "How did you happen to notice that the dinghy was missing, Lorell?"

"I . . . I just did, that's all," Lorell said nervously.

"Maybe you noticed it first because you already knew the cleat had been unhooked," Emma said slowly.

"You're crazy," Lorell protested. "I don't have to stand here and take this abuse." She spun around quickly to leave, but not before Emma saw the fear in her eyes.

Flash looked from Emma to his retreating girlfriend, then back at Emma. "Lorell wouldn't do something like that," Flash said.

Emma raised her eyebrows and just stared at Flash. Maybe she couldn't prove it, but Lorell's reaction had confirmed her suspicion. She really believed that Lorell was capable of doing something that awful.

"So, gotta motor," Flash said, donning his movie-star-hip sunglasses. "I, uh, I really am glad you guys are okay, ya know?" he said gruffly. "Later."

"So, that's everything," Carrie said to Graham as she concluded her story about what was going on with the *Rock On* interview. "I believe Faith is planning to make you look really bad in her article, and Flash has the photos to back her up."

Graham ran his hand over his face. He looked pale and tired and suddenly old, not at all like a famous rock star.

"Yeah, well, I shouldn't be surprised, should I?" Graham said. "Claudia kept trying to tell me, but I just didn't want to believe it." He looked out at the water. "That's what drugs can do to you, Carrie. They mess with your mind. I've got some fierce denial going on. "I've been under a lot of pressure lately. But doing drugs is no way to deal with it." He shook his head slowly. "I'm sorry, Carrie," he said. "I'm sorry to disappoint you like this."

Carrie blushed. "What are you going to do?" she asked.

"I hope I'm going to get my butt into a clinic where I can get some help," Graham said, "but I'd be lying if I told you I knew for sure that I had the strength to do it."

"You kicked drugs before," Carrie reminded him. "I know you can do it again.

Besides," she added softly, "your kids need you."

"Yeah, my kids," Graham said thoughtfully. After a pause he went on. "Thanks for the vote of confidence," he said, attempting a smile. "Hell, I don't know, maybe I wanted to get caught so I'd be forced to do something about it."

"If there's anything I can do to help . . ." Carrie said.

"Thanks," Graham said, "but this is one of those gigs where I guess I'm just gonna have to help myself."

On the other side of the deck, Sam stood talking to Chad. Out of the corner of her eye she saw Johnny Angel near the stairs, talking with his ex-girlfriend, Linda. Johnny looked over at Sam, but Linda grabbed his arms and said something. She looked angry. Johnny said something back to Linda, and then he walked over to Sam. Chad saw Johnny coming, and he diplomatically walked away.

"Hi," Johnny said quietly.

"Hi," Sam said.

"So, you gave everyone quite a scare," Johnny said. "I'm glad you're okay."

"Thanks," Sam said tersely.

"You're still mad at me," Johnny stated in a low voice.

"Does it matter?"

"It matters to me," Johnny said.

"Why, does everyone have to love you?" Sam spat out.

"No, everyone doesn't have to love me," Johnny said evenly. "I just hoped maybe we could be friends."

"Well, we can't," Sam answered. "Go back to Linda."

Sam started to walk away, but Johnny touched her arm gently. "Hey, I don't seem to be doing a very good job of this," he said bemusedly. "What I want to do is apologize to you."

"You do?" Sam asked.

"Yeah. I, uh, I kind of misread your signals or something. I didn't mean to . . . you know, do anything that you didn't want to do."

"I did want to," Sam admitted in a low voice. "I'm not going to lie about it. But the fact of the matter is, I don't know you and you don't know me. I just thought you were cute, and I liked the idea that you were this big rock star."

"There's nothing wrong with that," Johnny said with a smile.

"You can't fall in love with an idea," Sam said. "I'd rather wait for the real thing."

Johnny nodded and stared out at the water. "Cool," he said. "That's the only way it really means anything, anyway."

"So, um, good-bye," Sam said as she started to leave. "Good luck with your career and everything."

"Good luck with yours, too!" Johnny called after her. "Hey, Sam!" he said after a moment.

"What?" she said, turning around.

"I'm doing a gig in Orlando in January. Maybe you could show me around Disney World."

Sam smiled. "Maybe you could teach me how to do that triple spin you do," she called back.

"It's a deal," Johnny said.

"Ditto," said Sam with a grin.

"*There* you are," Carrie said when she saw Sam. She had located her cameras and slung them around her neck. "I'm beat. Are you ready to go?"

Sam nodded. "Where's Emma?"

"Right here," Emma said. "I want to go

back to the hotel and sleep for about a day."

"Me, too," Sam said. "But first I want to eat two of every single item on the room service menu."

Everyone was starting to leave the ship. Various people hugged the girls as they drifted off to their cars. Faith O'Connor came up to Emma and gave her her card. "I overheard you telling Chad what happened during the storm. What you did is nothing short of a miracle, and I think it would make a great first-person story for *Rock On*. Call me if you're interested."

Emma tore Faith's card into little bits when they got into their rented car. "That's my opinion of Faith O'Connor," Emma said.

"Well, she's right about one thing," Carrie said as she started up the car. "What you did *was* nothing short of a miracle."

"Oh, I don't know," Emma said. "I just happened to be the one who knew something about sailing."

"Don't you dare put down what you did!" Sam said. "You did something no snotty, spoiled rich girl could have ever done, got that?"

"I'm trying to," Emma said with a small smile.

"The Peace Corps would be lucky to get you," Carrie said vehemently.

"Right!" Sam agreed. "And just to show you the kind of friend I am, I'm willing to watch over your trust fund, your wardrobe, and your new car while you're off doing good for the downtrodden."

"Gee, Sam, you're a wonderful human being," Emma said solemnly.

"Not to mention a great humanitarian," Carrie added.

"Sure, I'm practically walking perfection," Sam agreed. "But you know what I have that's coolest of all?"

"What's that?" Carrie asked.

"The two greatest friends in the world."

They all smiled at one another. Sam cranked up the tunes and they headed down the open road.

More Sunset Island fun is on the way....
Look for SUNSET SECRETS in April!

Carrie, Emma, and Sam are hitting the highways. It's spring break and they're on their way to a mega party on beautiful Sunset Island. But will they make it on time? Surprises keep cropping up at every bend of the road, and somebody is not telling something!

by Cherie Bennett

When Emma, Sam, and Carrie spend the summer working as au pairs on a resort island, they quickly become allies in adventure!

__SUNSET ISLAND   0-425-12969-1/$3.50
__SUNSET KISS   0-425-12899-7/$3.50
__SUNSET DREAMS   0-425-13070-3/$3.50
__SUNSET FAREWELL   0-425-12772-9/$3.50

Join Emma, Sam, and Carrie when they get together again—for the ultimate winter break!

__SUNSET REUNION 0-425-13318-4/$3.50